LORD BENNETT, OF ASHWOOD HALL

The Wanderer

M.A. Grant

LORD BENNETT OF ASHWOOD HALL
The Wanderer

Copyright © by M.A. Grant and associates, 2024

First edition July 2024

ISBN: 979-8-9910972-1-5 [Paperback]

Illustrations and design by M.A. Grant

"The cover should be something green. Something beautiful, something living; a moth should do nicely."

For dear Michael Bennett: the only man I've ever loved.

I

Lord Samuel Bennett of Ashwood Hall was wasting away due to blood cancer at only forty-five years old, and very little could be done. Within months, he had a cough that would not subside, and he would not eat. He had lost so much weight that his once sturdy and rugged physique was now pale and withered, and his face had become a thin, translucent yellowing sheet pulled taut over his skull.

He was only awake for maybe six hours in a day, and the few servants left were always tending to him. He called his one son Michael near to him whenever he was lucid. Sometimes, he rambled about better days. Other times, he simply gazed at the patterns in the wallpaper. Michael sat for as long as he was wanted.

The last piece of information his father gave him was the address of Dr. Henry T. Webb, an acquaintance from his military service. At Lord Bennett's feeble request, a servant presented Michael with an envelope containing the last letter sent to his father from his old friend, in which he lamented his sickness and affirmed that his son was always free to seek him in his time of need.

Lord Bennett tried to reach a weak, trembling hand up to his face, but he was too feeble to do it on his own. It was a chore for him just to focus his flaming red eyes. Michael took his hand and held it up for him, though it was marred by lesions that looked painful, and he was hesitant to touch it.

"Michael, my son," he rasped through coughing fits, the effort of which made his blotchy lips crack. "Beautiful child… you must continue as you always have, whatever happens next. I have brought a most stouthearted young man into the world. I shall pass on with no regrets. Live your life that you may do the same. Promise me, boy."

He was lying. His father had a heart and a brain, and no man with half of each could truly die with no regrets. It stung him, but he did not have it in him to say it, so he silently affirmed his words.

"What! What!" Lord Bennett called out weakly but wildly. "I cannot hear you, Michael… speak up…"

"I promise, father…" he relented.

"My son… " he continued to mumble feverishly. "My boy… the joy of my life…"

Michael never doubted that his father loved him, but he was never the sort to make his feelings known very often. Hearing those words, even if they were the fragmented rambling of a man in his death throes, caused a swelling tightness in his chest. As much as he wanted, he could not cough, pant, or wail to relieve that pressure. It nearly suffocated him.

He put his hand back down, but Michael wasn't ready to let go.

At two o'clock in the morning, on May 15, 1887, he breathed his last soon after his son had dozed off in his old bedside chair, and he was awoken by the servants' strangled, anguished sobs, and wet feet.

"Oh, he's dead! He's dead!" the chambermaid dropped the bucket of water she was carrying as she cried out into the dark gallery, and Abraham the butler scolded her for causing a scene, lest she upset "the young Master."

He then dismissed her from the room to fetch the physician, who confirmed everyone's fears.

Michael had already broken his promise.

He was laid to rest beside his wife Mary, with a small shiny stone between them. They buried him in his old uniform. It was disturbingly loose.

The only attendees of Lord Samuel Bennett's funeral were his servants, a few military officers, and of course, his son. There was not much left of the Bennett family, save for a handful of cousins that Michael had never met. He was sure that his father once mentioned a sister, but he didn't know where to look, or if he even wanted to…

As it was, he was the sole beneficiary of Ashwood Hall.

He returned to the mansion after the brief service. Right away, the servants began calling him "Lord Bennett." It startled him. They asked about him, and tried to feed him and draw him a warm bath. He could scarcely find the words to answer them. Abraham read to him and kissed his brow, and he slept in the library so that he didn't need to pass Samuel Bennett's chamber.

He received his father's title and station, his property, and his debt. Ever since the rise in industry and urbanisation, the land simply wasn't generating enough of a profit to be sustainable anymore, as most of the labourers had died off or moved to the cities. Additionally, it seemed that his father, while a mostly decent and honest landlord, was rather negligent with his finances.

Michael was not aware of any of this until after his death, and had only mourned his father for three weeks when he received notice that somebody would be going to prison if those debts were not paid one way or another.

"But it is no longer lawful to imprison somebody for their debts," he tried to plead his own case to the uniformed men breathing in his face.

"Ah, but you see, there are exceptions, when one is able to pay, and I daresay, there are some things in this world that you can offer up. Wouldn't you agree?"

As he spoke, one of the men reached a hand out and tenderly ran his finger along the watch chain peeking out from Michael's waistcoat. He shifted on his feet to conceal the shudder that ran through him.

In the midst of the grief and confusion, he quickly grew desperate. As despaired as he was, debtor's prison at only nineteen years of age was a sickening thought.

Anything that was officially owned by the crown was seized: most of the village and farmland. Even then, there were debts owed to many parties.

He sold the home of his ancestors, and nearly everything tied to it. Its assets had been gathered by countless generations, over the course of roughly four hundred years, and the great Ashwood house was nearly as old as the village itself. He was born there, along with his father, and it was his inheritance, entrusted to him less than a month ago.

And he sold it.

It was enough of a profit to pay off his father's debts and keep him well for a while. The best thing to do would be to save up whatever he could and start with a fresh slate… not that he knew how. The person he wanted to ask most of all was out of reach.

As he signed it over to some nouveau riche Americans, he wondered whether or not he should have just charmed one of those oil magnates into giving him his daughter and a sizeable dowry besides, in exchange for a title that didn't mean anything overseas. It would have only cost his dignity and his freedom.

After he had vomited into an alleyway outside of the solicitor's office, he made his way back home to pack up what he planned to keep. He did not have long until he would be evicted.

It was hard to separate the essentials from the sentimental relics. Even on hunting trips and wilderness outings, he was infamous for only

ever packing way too much, or hardly anything
at all.

 He tried to keep his finery minimal and
practical: his father's watch and good knives, his
mother's locket, and a set of fine handkerchiefs.
He then packed his shaving box, his rifle and
pistol, and not a great deal of clothing, as even
his fine suits were sold. Abraham supervised his
endeavours, to ensure that he packed correctly.

Three other servants stayed behind to tend to
him in those last days. He only remembered to
eat because someone cooked.

At night, he paced many laps through the
spacious corridors and looked up at the starlight
through those grand windows for as long as he
could.

It was a cold and merciless feeling, watching
Abraham shut the door behind him. This would
possibly be the last time they'd speak, and he
had been an invaluable comfort in that interval,
but he kept his goodbyes brief to remain
composed.

For some reason that may have been pride, he
decided to depart early in the morning, thinking
it was better to leave on his own accord than to
draw out his stay and be cast out. This sentiment
was even stronger than his attachment to his

dwelling. He had to remind himself continuously that it was not his, to forcefully snap the cord that fastened him to its walls.

The gate shut, and then Michael was homeless. Thus began his journey south into town. He ventured forthwith, with all that he could carry that had not been liquidated, and the letter with Dr. Webb's address on the envelope.

He strayed from the cobbled streets and walked through the fields, for he did not want to be seen. It was a beautiful and mild early summer morning, still as the cemetery at the village's end, where his father now rested with many ancestors before him.

The silence was broken by the cooing of a lone dove. He looked up and watched as it alighted on a twisted branch above him. Its fat little body swayed and bobbed on the thin shoot, and it continued to sing without fear.

Michael had no such finesse. In watching, he was not looking where he stepped, and he stumbled over the tree's thick roots, spilling to the ground with his bags clattering on top of him.

There, he wept.

And as he wept, he thought of all he could have done instead of selling the property, had he only allowed himself to reflect in due time, only sought more answers. It was too late now.

He did not know for how long he lay. Maybe he was hoping to die and be consumed by the earth. The sun beat down on his head when the world started to move again. So it was close to noon.

He peeled himself off of the ground, with grass and damp hair forming a plaster over one side of his face, and a terrible fatigue from the effort of weeping. Some unknown force had him on his feet and walking mechanically. Whether it was his own will, or God's, he did not know.

So absently did he walk that he did not feel his ankles throbbing. Bugs that had gotten hold of him as he wallowed in the grass were still crawling in his hair and on his clothes, and he was endlessly picking them off. Perhaps he could have hired a ride into town, but he was in such a difficult mood that morning, that he just never seemed to do anything the easy way.

By the time he made it to the outskirts of town, it was in the middle of the afternoon. There was no time to stop now, so he satiated his hunger by picking berries from the briar that skirted the road.

His journey was not over yet.

Boarding a train further south, Michael finally had a moment to rest his limbs, and have his first drink of water that day. There was a little moth that he missed while plucking the crawling things off; it emerged from his lapel when he'd already departed. When he was little, he used to caress them until his father told him not to; their wings were too tender. The surprise raised his spirits for just a moment. He scooped it up and put it in his shaving box until he reached his stop, so that nobody would accidentally crush it.

He did not feel it would do him any good to reflect further on what he was leaving behind. It was too bitter. Luckily for him, fatigue seized him before his thoughts could, and after a dreamless but fitful slumber, he arrived at his destination in the evening.

It was a modest and quiet-looking village, with not a lot of people out and about under the streetlights. The dim lights cast ghostly impressions upon the buildings, and all that spread around it was perfectly still. Grand, rolling hills enclosed it for miles on all sides. The roads were in a state of disrepair. It was a wonder that this place even had a train terminal.

Primitive as it appeared to be, there was no evidence of rampant crime. He only heard low murmurs and creatures of the night, occasionally punctuated by a slamming door somewhere.

Did he like the look of it? Not necessarily, but he did not feel threatened.

He decided he should perhaps stay at an inn until morning instead of dropping in unannounced at this hour. Moreover, even holding himself upright was a tremendous effort, for he had fallen asleep with his neck lodged between two cushions and bent back almost to the point of breaking.

The sole inn on the street had only two rooms; that's how small this town was. The innkeeper, a Mr. Briggs, was pleasant enough, though a bit puzzled that a man of supposedly high status had arrived in a place like this alone, filthy, and unattended, carrying his own luggage— and so much of it. Hopefully he did not seem suspicious.

Still, it was so heavenly just to stretch out! He lay himself down on a bed with no curtains, in a room with no carpet, and tried to sleep again.

When Michael closed his eyes, he only saw his father's sunken skull face, and it stared at him balefully, silently accusing him of treachery.

He awoke drenched in sweat, and it took him some minutes to remember where he was. After he came to terms with reality, he washed himself, and rediscovered the moth in his shaving kit, miraculously still alive. He released it through the window.

"Farewell, small fellow! So sorry that we've both been displaced. I hope we can make a living here."

He finished shaving, and set out without taking breakfast, certainly not the mystery gruel that was served at the inn. In truth, he felt too ill to eat, giddy about this new chapter, and sick with suppressed emotions.

The look of his father just before he passed may never leave him.

That morning was overcast and pleasantly cool, and workers were now ambling about. He felt out of place in his finely tailored attire, and it did not help that they looked him up and down with a puzzled and scrutinising eye as he passed.

This was possibly, in part, due to his stature. At just over six feet tall and with considerable breadth of frame, he was certainly a bit larger than the average fellow. He was bigger than his father but smaller than his grandfather Nathaniel Bennett, who was monstrously tall by all accounts. He had much ado to avoid trampling the hoards of children gathered on the walkway.

He took out the letter and looked at it again. The ink on half of the address had been soaked and smeared, and he did not have the foresight to commit it to memory yesterday. He hadn't even written before coming. He really just made one misstep after another. Surely— hopefully— Dr. Webb was a well-known presence in this village.

As he put the letter back, a piercing yelp like a stray cat cut through the peaceful morning bustle.

It seemed he'd stepped on some little toes.

"Watch it, you ape!" a reedy voice called behind in a most unrefined accent.

He turned. It was no cat, but a young girl probably no more than ten, in a shapeless frock and black stockings. With her features pinched into a perpetual scowl, she truly had the most disagreeable face he'd ever seen on a child. The ensemble was framed by a mess of loose flaxen hair.

"Oh, I'm terribly sorry, little Miss. Is your foot alright?"

"Who're you?"

"Well, I'm Michael Bennett, formerly of Ashwood Hall," Michael put on the smoothest and most gracious tone he could muster, as he realised this was his chance to ask around. "Say, I wonder if you know of a Dr. Henry Webb living near here?"

"That's my uncle. What do you need him for?"

"He is! Well, how wonderful! Could you perhaps show me where he lives?"

"I can. But it'll cost you."

How annoying. And she meant it, too. He didn't want to be stiffed by this little yob, especially since she looked well-fed and clean enough.

But he was growing impatient, and it wouldn't hurt to relinquish a bit of pocket change. Besides, he'd already stomped on some of her toes, so perhaps a little compensation was in order.

"Very well, name your price," he drew out his purse.

She tapped her chin with one hand and swished her skirt with the other, seeming to take great delight in making him wait.

"Three shillings will do nicely, I think."

His heart sank into his stomach. That was almost all of the coins he had. He was not accustomed to carrying much on his person.

"Three shillings, my—!" Michael caught himself.

"Your what!" the ankle biter demanded. "That's breadcrumbs to a prissy fop like you! Cough it up or be on your way!"

"Now you wait a moment!" he took out just one coin and held it up to her. "If I give you all of it now, you're liable to run off without giving me my dues. You can have the rest when you escort me to your uncle's house."

"Why should I trust you?"

He was one hair away from cutting his losses and asking around town, even if it may have taken longer.

"I give you my word, as a gentleman of Ashwood," said he.

Former gentleman of Ashwood, that is.

"Fine," she held out a hand for her payment and marched off without waiting for him.

Not that it was difficult to match her pace, as she only came up just above his waist, tiny thing that she was. Unfortunately, this made it easy to lose track of her on the busy pavement, and he could not take up a leisurely stride until they were past the semi urban sprawl and into the rural expanses just outside of town.

Tall, stately farmhouses stood close to the road and within decent shouting distance of one another, so it was not a completely desolate location. The fields were lush with robust crops, and grazing animals peppered the landscape.

The little brat was not content to simply guide him to the house; on the contrary, she pointed out and explained every detail of the land from the ancient infrastructure to the grass, as if he was a complete moron. He pretended to pay attention for as long as he could.

Unlike their city counterparts, country folk usually made up for their low, coarse nature with hospitality and deference. Hopefully she was an exception.

Dr. Webb's residence was a two storey brick structure at the far end of a crumbling avenue. The facade was neat and respectable, bordered with bright flowers and blossoming cherry trees. Behind it was a decent plot of land, a bare wooden barn, and a little shed of some kind.

They stepped over the stile and up the walkway, and his guide let herself inside without knocking.

"ALMA!" she screeched into the hall and stomped her way in without wiping her feet.

She waited a moment.

"Smells like she's making breakfast."

Indeed, a pleasant blend of warmth and enticing smells wafted around him as he entered the kitchen behind her. The interior was minimally decorated and composed of modern board and plaster.

Michael saw a small woman —whom he guessed was Alma— with her head bent over an old stove at the far end of the room. She was clad in a dark grey wrapper, and a loose knot of tawny hair was arranged at the base of her neck. A kettle and a crackling iron pan perched on the stovetop under her hands.

"There's a queer man come for Uncle Henry!" the child shrieked again.

"Let him come in and sit down, then," the lady answered in a low and mild tone of voice with her back to them still, not wishing to take her eyes off of her task, it seemed.

As was his habit, he would not take a seat until he was acknowledged face to face, so he stood over the table and waited, with hat and letter in hand.

"I brought you all the way here, Mister," his companion tugged his sleeve. "You'd better pay up."

"Yes, yes, of course," all too eager to be rid of her, Michael produced the money and poured it into her beckoning hand.

The woman turned at last, and a broad set of eyeglasses caught the light shining through the window.

She was very pale and almost as small as the little girl, but unmistakably matured in shape. Everything about her seemed quite delicate and miniscule, save for the squared shoulders, prominent forehead, and most notably, the eyes: they were large and dark, and drawn wide as she registered this strange, hulking man in her kitchen.

He remembered his manners:

"Good day, Miss, I'm Michael Bennett, of Ashwood Hall," he bowed his head and waved the letter he was holding.

This revelation raised her features even more. Apparently, he was expected.

"Oy, you!" the little swindler yanked at his clothes to make him face her. "What about me! A gentleman is supposed to bow to all ladies!"

"Go find me one, then," Michael tugged his coattail out of her hands. Just as she started to get riled up, she was stopped short.

"Ida, why don't you go get Uncle Henry from upstairs? I think he's in his study," Alma pointed down the hall and gave her a little tap on the back.

She seemed to put the little rat under a spell, as she huffed and scurried off without protest.

What a wholly unpleasant child. He heard her clopping up the stairs when he turned his attention back to Miss Alma. From the side, he saw that her nose was long, straight, and sharp, like a bird's beak.

"Be seated, please," she gestured to the table and went to heave the kettle off of the heat. "I've just finished breakfast. Is there anything I can get you, sir?"

"Well, if you have a little water, that would be just fine. Preferably clean water, if possible."

She turned to him and stared for a moment with a perplexing expression, but brought him a glass of water without a word, plunking it down on the table so harshly that he cringed at the impact.

He examined it and took a cautious sip. It was slightly bitter, alkaline perhaps, but probably harmless.

He examined the hostess, as well. Her movements were calculated, and as slight and tender as her frame, even over a menial task. Even her speech was singular, almost rhythmic; she pronounced each syllable roundly and sharply, with intent.

Her demeanour did not quite line up with her apparent method of cooking: that is, to scoot the heap around all together in one massive pan. He smelled bacon, butter, and eggs, and saw her toss sliced bread into the leftover grease, which there was plenty of. Just now it occurred to him that he'd not eaten anything but a handful of berries the past two days, and the smell of meat made him realise how faint he was. He wondered how that mess would taste.

He wondered, as well, about this lady's relation to Dr. Webb and little Ida. He guessed she was a nurse or maid in the house, but her hands were too soft and pretty.

"Madam, are you Ida's sister, perhaps?" Michael chose a more polite inquiry than to charge her with being a servant.

"No, sir, she is my cousin, and Dr. Webb is my father," she was busy setting out plates. "Are you sure you won't have some food? There's plenty."

He was not aware that the doctor had any children, but he was certainly aware that he was starving.

"Now that you mention it, I think I'll have just a bit of toast, if you please."

As she served him and laid out other plates, he noticed she often kept her eyes fixed downward, and only met his for a fleeting moment under fluttering lashes. She seemed a timid creature, yet with enough of a presence to temper her wayward cousin in an instant.

Two sets of footsteps came tapping into the kitchen. They belonged to Ida, and a man of about fifty strolling close behind her. Above his neatly trimmed greying beard, he had a pair of deep-set eyes behind round lenses. His hair was a clean, horizontal sweep above his forehead. He wore a brown tweed jacket and dark trousers, and held a pipe to his lips. If any man had the true essence of a healer, it was him. Michael liked him immediately.

"Papa, did Ida tell you this man Mr. Bennett is here for you?" Alma approached the table and pulled out chairs.

"She did not tell me quite the same, she told me that 'some dandy with a long coat' was in the kitchen," his voice was deep, gentle, and rich as fresh cream, with a hint of some Northern accent. It made Michael ache for his own father.

He stood and reached out his hand.

"Sir, it is a pleasure to make your acquaintance. My name is Michael Bennett. You knew my father, and I have one of your letters as proof."

The doctor took his hand in a warm and firm grip.

"I did indeed know your father, yes, he was a good man," from there, his smooth voice began to crack, and his eyes glistened behind his glasses. "I cannot tell you how I suffered when I prepared to visit him, and was told he had already passed, but I'm so pleased to meet you, boy. You look just like him, I say."

"He passed peacefully and with dignity," Michael replied, and thus they were both lying to each other. "And he told me I should come here and be among friends, good sir."

"Well, sit, sit!" Dr. Webb gestured to the chair Michael had risen from and seated himself next to him. "Ah, Alma, my girl, this man's father was a good friend of mine, you know, and a nobleman at that! We ought to treat him well, so don't poison this one," he chuckled at his own jest. "Would you take some coffee?"

"No, thank you, I'm alright with what I have."

Of course, Ida was not still and silent this whole time. She was tripping round the room in her own little dream world, ploughing through anyone and anything that stood in her way, bouncing a rubber ball off of the walls and floor until her cousin put a stop to her.

"Sit down and have breakfast, Ida," Alma poured milk into a mug for her and beckoned her to the table, making sure she was seated and devouring her meal before she herself chased after the ball left rolling into another room.

Michael waited until everybody sat and settled in before he began eating. He'd never had bread fried on a stovetop in butter and pork fat. Though he was sceptical at first, it was unlike anything he'd tasted before. It had a delightful crust, and the flavour was aromatic and permeating, as if the bread itself was enriched with meat. He was instantly convinced that this was the only proper way to prepare toast. Perhaps it was just his appetite talking, but he believed this was rich enough to be a meal of its own.

Dr. Henry Webb apparently loved to talk, especially to tell stories. He lit his pipe and was quick to tell Michael all that he had seen and books he'd collected during his stay in India for military service, as well as his other travels. It was fascinating to hear the experiences of the older generations, and his interest was piqued at the mention of rifles, because he had the opportunity to share his own stories about his hunting trips. Of course, they were nothing spectacular to a seasoned traveller and military man, but the doctor still took a passive and patient pleasure in listening.

Miss Alma ate quite quickly, staring out the window, saying very little except to occasionally put in a comment on her father's stories, refill somebody's cup, or answer to Ida when she spoke off to the side.

Ida finished eating the fastest, as she had no grasp on the concept of moderation, and she tried to bolt out the door, but Alma grabbed ahold of her to readjust her sash, smooth her untamed hair, and drop a few kisses onto her wretched face before escorting her out.

"Ida is your niece, yes?" Michael asked now that the subject could not hear, nor interrupt. "Does she live with you?"

"She may as well," Dr. Webb took a long draught of his pipe before he continued. "She is my wife's sister's daughter. Her father died when she was only a wee thing, and her mother… well, she lives nearby, though she's not exactly a consistent influence. As you may have noticed, she's not a particularly well-mannered child."

"Really!" he pretended this was news to him.

"Yes, indeed. I'm afraid there's no end to what she might do for want of attention, but she has always been a sort of pet to Alma. I'm counting on her to make her into a fine young lady."

"Ah, I understand," Michael studied Alma as she returned, trying to find in her the qualities of refinement. Her hands were folded demurely on the table, but he saw bits of hair had come loose and now hung down around her face, and she didn't seem to mind. Despite being clad in plain work clothes, she had a shining shell brooch pinned above her apron. He also recalled that she'd never formally introduced herself to him. The search was inconclusive. He found her full

of strange contradictions. Maybe he should
become better acquainted with her.

There was a lot of food on her plate for
somebody her size. He watched curiously, to see
if she would finish it. She resumed eating and
indeed cleaned her plate, then helped herself to
more fried eggs and filled her mug with milk.

"Eat as much as you want," Dr. Webb told her.
"Your brother will not be home until this
evening."

It seemed to be only Alma, her father, and a yet
unnamed son in the house, so Michael cautioned
to ask:

"Sir, is your wife still living?"

"She is," he nodded, and feathery wisps of
smoke rose from a large gap in his top teeth.
"Though we are separated. My children are
grown, I have that one," he pointed his pipe at
Alma. "And I have a son, James, but they travel
between the two of us often."

Though he seemed to be at ease, Michael didn't
ask what circumstances had rent him from his
spouse, lest he strike some ill chord.

"Now, Mr. Bennett," Dr. Webb set his finished
pipe down on the table. "I'm sure you did not

come all this way just to humour a lonely old
man. Was there something you needed?"

The conversation had been so intriguing and
delightful thus far, truly the best he'd had in
months, that he had nearly forgotten the reason
he came in the first place.

"Well, yes, actually," he admitted. "I don't know
if my father ever told you, but he accumulated a
great debt before he died," this next part, he
needed to take a breath to gather himself. "I was
forced to sell the old estate in order to pay them
off, and now I have no home, no relatives who
would claim me."

"And you're hoping to seek refuge here?"

"Yes, sir, but more so, I was hoping I could be of
use to you. I'm not particularly skilled in any
trade, but I believe I could be put to work
running errands or doing manual labour. I'm
quite capable, I should think. I'd like to work for
you, if I may."

A broad grin spread over the doctor's face,
bearing his straight and square, tobacco-stained
teeth. This answer pleased him.

"Good on you for wanting to earn your keep,
boy. Well, I reckon I could put you to work, and
I like you, so I'll tell you what," he laced his

fingers under his chin. "You won't have to pay for your meals. I am happy to feed you, and you will eat with us. You will sleep in the outbuilding for now. There is a little stove, and a nice cot can be set up. If you agree to these arrangements, we'll discuss your wages."

Being banished to the outhouse sounded degrading indeed. The idea of cramming himself into such a pitiful wooden crate of an enclosure made his skin crawl.

Furthermore, he fancied being somebody's errand boy was little better than being a shoe shiner or some sort of *male chambermaid*, but he did not feel he was in any position to argue, so he had no choice but to set his teeth and accept these conditions.

They shook hands once again, and he was now a working man.

Michael needed only to collect his luggage that was being held at the inn, and then he was put to work that same day, doing essentially anything the good doctor requested of him. That first week, he posted mail, cleaned his old rifles, and filed papers in the study. He always had a lot of letters to collect and deliver. Dr. Webb continuously corresponded with many of his patients, particularly the ones he saw as infants.

Sometimes, Michael tended to the chickens and gathered up their eggs (when he could gather up the courage). They did not recognise him as a friend, and he started and dropped an egg when one of them snarled. They descended upon it with vigour, causing him to give a rather unmanly cry of alarm and scamper away. Thankfully, nobody saw this happen.

Aside from that, it was all very easy: a little too easy. Hopefully, this would not be the extent of his labour. He wanted to be challenged in some way.

At night, he knelt and prayed, because that was what he was raised to do, and then he arranged himself as comfortably as he could on a straw cot that barely accommodated his bulk, watching spiders crawl on his belongings.

He got used to the place quickly. He did not come to *like* it; that was not the right word, but he adapted well enough. He ended up running a lot of errands that involved going into town. For a man who liked to talk and travel, the doctor sure didn't interact with other people very often.

The locals were pleasant and welcoming, if a bit base and alien to him. They liked to talk about local politics, good drink, and what they were going to have for supper that evening.

"Good drink" was quite subjective. At the inn's tavern, he requested a mulled wine (unorthodox in summer, but he had an intense craving to satisfy) and the closest they had was cider. It was warm, not hot. He was disappointed, but accepted it with grace, and paid with his last bit of coin.

Children were easy to please, for the most part. He became their hero just by getting a kite out of a tree for them, or giving them a half penny, which he didn't mind doing when they asked nicely. They were carefree and mischievous, unburdened by rigid expectations and obligations beyond fetching water and gathering kindling. Sometimes he kicked a ball back to them if it rolled his way, and for a moment, he felt like a child again. If he still had any of his toys, he'd have gladly shared them. He never used them as a child anyway, except when he was forbidden to go outside during inclement weather, and had absolutely nothing else to do.

The women? They were tall, plump, and pretty, and most were groomed well even for their want of finery. It seemed to be consistent among every caste and race that women loved to be beautiful, and loved beauty. He saw them eyeing his fine clothes and his hair (indeed, he had a full head of wavy auburn hair that he took great pride in). When he spoke to them, they took notice of his "pretty" accent. Even in plain work attire, he exposed himself as an outsider the moment he opened his mouth.

Despite all of this, their wit and ideas were every measure as common as their (only slightly) rougher male counterparts. He never fancied himself good at talking to girls, as it was. But why did that matter to him? If he was to desire a bride, he'd likely not be choosing from this breed— meaning no offence to them or their charms, of course.

It occurred to him only just now to ask himself why he had adopted such a low-born existence when he still had decent means tucked away in a bank vault, and could use them to travel the world if he pleased.

Well, he had decided to submit to this life for now, and save every penny he earned, so that he may one day buy back the house he was raised in, even if it took a lifetime. This was his one driving force that coaxed him out of bed in those days.

What measure was a lifetime at nineteen? Did he understand the gravity of this vow?

He was quite fond of Henry Webb. His kindness seemed to stem from a solitary and mundane life, and desire for new faces. Though he claimed his wanderlust had been satiated long ago, there was always a restless gleam in his eyes as he told his tales. With him, Michael partook in his first cigar, a milestone he anticipated.

Unsavoury details aside, he was not made to be a smoker, and his dinner did not taste nearly as good coming up as it did going down. Dr. Webb finished his cigar for him.

Michael's desire for more stimulating work was fulfilled in July, when the alfalfa ripened. He was charged with reaping, processing, and hauling the hay, and it was hard work that tickled his nose and itched his arms. Though he was a robust fellow who had been put through many sports in his time, he found the occupation challenging, as he had the muscle, but not the skill. Gentry may have called it "unskilled" labour, but it required a measure of dexterity that he needed time to master. Sometimes, he was more of a hindrance than a helper.

At first, he insisted upon wearing a coat, and no hat, though no other men did so, and they warned him. He would have felt exposed, even in the presence of only men, but suppose a woman passed on the road and saw his damp shirt clinging to his body! He simply did not like hats, so he kept his hair fairly long to shield his ears and neck, but with the sun bearing down on him for hours without end, it was not enough

protection. His coat made his movements stiff
and difficult. Within half a day's work, nature
had humbled him, and he returned after dinner
disrobed, with a broad straw hat.

He often did this task alongside Dr. Webb's son,
James. Like his sister, he mostly kept to himself,
aside from occasionally correcting him and
mumbling under his breath about how Michael
was unfit for honest work, though he still
summoned him to assist in the climbing and
heavy lifting. On very rare occasions, Michael
had to pick up snakes and move them out the
way. He did not mind it, though many of the
workers were fearful. A friend of his father's had
a fondness for exotic reptiles and kept quite an
extensive collection, so he was accustomed to
them, and even enjoyed them: much more than
any of the field cats.

Once he'd gotten into the rhythm of it, the work
was exhilarating. The rustic and unpolished
meals he ate now had a charm on him, and even
going to bed sore, with tingling, watery eyes was
a welcome feeling. It made his repose all the
more satisfying. Ida was ever-present at least
every other day, often munching on sweets she'd
bought with his three shillings, sometimes
prodding him while he tried to work. Each time
he saw her, he meditated on how she was the
perfect height to be kicked in the sternum. Is this

how people thought of him when he was a little boy?

It was difficult to believe he was living such a luxurious life only last spring, even if the wealth was a lie. For better or worse, he felt himself to be a completely different man now.

III

Eventually, the grasses ceased to irritate his face so much, and his features were no longer florid and puffy in the evening. This mattered a great deal to him. He still had his vanity in spite of it all. His hands, however, had become tough as leather, and similar in colour, as he no longer burned in the sun, and had been baked a deep, ruddy bronze.

The field he sheared gradually rolled into a wide hill upon which he could see all that spread around him. Alma could often be seen from there, picking ripening cherries, throwing feed to the chickens, drawing water from the well, or laying out scraps for stray cats and patting their velvety heads. Michael even saw her playing with Ida once or twice. He observed that Ida cleaved to her side as if she was her mother, and extended no such devotion to anyone else, not even her uncle. Alma clung to her and kissed her even when reprimanding her. Ida would eventually run off and leave her, drawn away by anything from other children to a bird.

Sometimes when she was alone, Alma would lapse into wandering listlessly, seeming to dream as she paced with her eyes fixed on the horizon, until some stimulus roused her and she resumed her task. He wondered what visions she conjured up in her mind's eye that could captivate her so thoroughly. On several occasions, he, himself, would fall into a trance while watching her.

Her tendency to dream was particularly noticeable when she once asked him to help her in the kitchen: a request that petrified him, but it turned out that she only needed him to stir an egg mixture for her. Even he could do that. Just about anybody could do it, so for her to call upon him, there must have been no-one else available.

Michael rolled up his sleeves and set to work while she sliced walnuts. Unsure of how to fill in the silence, he tried to make pleasant conversation on his complete lack of knowledge in regards to cooking, and received only a few affirmative chirps as a response.

"I've only ever skinned and roasted game over a fire," he said, while watching carefully so as to not spill one drop. "My mother learned to cook while in India, and when I was sick, she'd make this curry that was so very spicy, it made my eyes and nose water! She claimed that it purged the sickness, and you would recover faster. Truthfully, I wish I knew how to make it…"

He looked over at Miss Alma to see if he was boring her, he saw she had lapsed into reverie, with her eyes fixed on his stirring and her knife floating over the cutting board. He called her name, and she started, blushed deeply, and lowered her head.

"I do have that effect on women," he told her. "I strike up a nice conversation, and they just go right to sleep!"

Miss Webb smiled, and as if he'd been bewitched, he had to smile, too.

"You can stop that now," she tapped on the bowl. "Thank you."

The mixture he'd beaten into stiff lumps became a collection of velvety sweets she packed up to bring to church. She left some as thanks for his help, and though they were made well, he did not enjoy the pillowy texture against his teeth. He still gladly ate what he was given.

As all good things must come to an end, the season of making hay and harvesting fruit had drawn to a close in September, and the reaping tools were retired. Then he was stagnant again.

He had a broad and practical hat for working outside, but some of his shirts did not hold up against the strain for very long. Seams were starting to come apart, and one of them had a noticeable tear down the left sleeve. He didn't realise it until he undressed one Saturday night, when his fingers caught the stray threads.

This really gnawed at him. Even as active as he was, he'd never worn through his clothes before, only outgrown them, or ruined them with mud, so this was not an issue he was used to being confronted with. He merely huffed about it and left the garments in a pile.

Sunday was his proper day of rest, and on this day, he could come and go from the house as he pleased.

Roaming the halls, he found nothing decorative in the house, except for many photographs on the walls. The doctor did say that he enjoyed having pictures taken, though Michael found very few of the man himself, but many of his children, and a dark-haired woman he guessed to be Mrs. Webb— she strongly resembled Alma Webb, but a bit more lithe and angular.

He ventured into the parlour to find something to amuse himself. Indoors was rarely exceptionally appealing to him, but the aesthetic of the room was welcoming enough. Brown, gold, and burgundy seemed to be the palette of choice for the furnishing, from the wallpaper and baseboards to the rug and the cushions lining the sofas. It offered a regal, yet warm and intimate air.

A skirted piano stood at the far end of the room, and there was plenty of music. He'd not practised in a long time, but he fancied he could still play an enjoyable tune without any egregious errors if he tried right that minute.

Some other day. His attention was captured by a tall mahogany shelf lined with a modest collection of books, in many different languages. He only knew French, German, some Spanish, and a negligent portion of Hindostanee, so his pickings of the foreign literature were slim. Dr. Webb's study had books on botany and lepidoptery, which were quite tempting, but he did not feel entitled to go upstairs and take them.

Voltaire's *Candide, ou l'Optimisme* stuck out to him. French philosophy was a favoured talking point in his former social circles, so the title was somewhat nostalgic. Despite this, he never developed a liking for it. In a sheltered and innocent upbringing such as his, satire did not suit his taste, and as things were, he didn't feel pressured to pretend it did. Since he'd never bothered to finish it and long forgotten it until now, he considered it a worthwhile read, and selected it from the shelf.

He'd just opened it up when he heard the parlour door creak ever so slightly, and he froze, as if he was not supposed to be there.

Michael turned and saw a slender hand reach inside before the rest of the person emerged. Those big, round almond eyes and rimless eyeglasses caught his attention immediately. She, too, froze when she saw he was looking directly at her, still in her good celadon dress for morning church. With the stiff ivory collar and pearly features above it, he was reminded of the lilies nodding their heads outside.

"Miss Webb!" he shut the book and folded his hands, and leaned forward in a sort of bowing gesture. "Did you need something?"

She became animated again when he called her name.

"Umm…" she hummed and produced a little parcel from behind her back. "Here, this is yours."

She set it on one of the side tables and slipped back into the hall, with a tread as soft and swift as that of the cats she was so fond of.

Now this was intriguing. He was not expecting a package.

After sliding *Candide, ou l'Optimisme* back into place, he approached and picked up the parcel. It was paper bound in ribbon, and its contents gave him a bit of a pleasant start.

He pulled out his shirts, cleaned and pressed, albeit a bit messily, but most notably of all, the seams had been repaired, and the one tear threaded over, almost as if it had never been there.

Almost. It was too imperfect to have been the work of a professional, yet it pleased him greatly, perhaps even more so than a hired hand. He tied the parcel back up in a much uglier knot than it previously had, and passed out of the parlour door to search for Alma.

But it seemed she had vanished from the house, and he did not see her out on the lawn, either. She had dissipated like vapour, a most ethereal thing she was! He was vexed at her for retreating so suddenly before he could even thank her.

Michael was not yet brave enough to go and ask Dr. Webb where he could find his daughter, and certainly wasn't about to go tapping on doors.

It turned out, he would not see her again for a fortnight, as she was visiting her mother and had taken Ida with her. It was just the men with the house to themselves, and he had ample time to ponder why it mattered so much to him that he had to wait to see her again. Maybe it was the mystery of it all. It was clear enough that she was at least a gentle being, but she was elusive, and he wanted so terribly to plumb the depths of a character that could have a genuine affection for whatever Ida was. As it was, the extent of their intercourse throughout the day was a polite nod in the hallway, or a plain and simple "thank you" for a delicious meal.

He loved a good puzzle, but half of him was worried that the singularity of her nature would be lost on him when he examined it further, thus he wondered whether or not he should keep her at a distance. That, he did not feel he could do.

It is a queer feeling, when somebody you'd gotten used to suddenly disappears. Their departure is often not realised right away or as a whole, but little things are missing, and those things start to pile up.

He did not hear her little songbird's warble of a laugh ringing over the lawn or through the hallway, be it an incredulous response to her cousin's lunacy, or a squeal of delight as she herded a litter of kittens into her lap.

Her absence was noticed for sure at supper, when he had his first taste of James's soggy, waxen roast potatoes and flavourless fried fish. In short: precisely how Michael expected a young bachelor to cook. Hardly a sumptuous repast, but as with most things, he'd learned to accept it for what it was with a little salt and a mind of gratitude. He didn't offer any criticism because he knew with certainty that he could do no better. He still said his thanks over his daily bread, as he was accustomed to doing, and could weather any hardship while he carried the hope of returning honour to his family.

Michael had not forgotten his father all this time, not for a moment. He'd simply been hard at work, and scarcely allowed himself the time to sit quietly with his thoughts. His father was always in the formula of his prayers, and he wore his old silken handkerchiefs around his neck every Sunday. It was comforting to brush his fingers over the fabric. He remembered his mother's locket, as well. She had passed away so long ago that it was one of his only relics of hers, therefore it was far too precious to wear, and stayed in its little lacquered casket in his trunk.

Abraham was also dearly missed, as he had worked for the family since Samuel was a young boy, and he was the closest thing that Michael had to a grandfather. Even though it could scarcely be helped, he was still struck with pangs of remorse for dismissing him the way

that he had, and wished to someday make
amends. There must have been a way to contact
him. He could perhaps sift through the copies of
legal documents that he had taken with him.

He now had steady wages: a scant thirty-five
shillings per week, but it was easy to save up
when his room and board was guaranteed. Every
bit he saved sent a thrill through his whole
frame, even if it meant maintaining such a low
standard of living.

IV

In the outskirts, this clean, pretty hamlet was
perfect to take long walks when he was not
running errands. Insects were bigger in the
south, and wildflowers were as fragrant as they
were abundant. The shorn fields wet with crystal
dew glittered all the colours of the rainbow in
the sunrise, and many different types of birds
awakened the sun with a swelling crescendo.

Michael wandered out until he found a
wonderful little stream, and while it was still
hot, he lay himself down in the muddy banks, in
all of his clothes, letting the plants and little
creatures tickle and pull at his hair. He preferred
cool running water over a warm bath at any
time. After his rejuvenating soak in the fountain
of youth, he squeezed the water out of his hair,

replaced his hat, and walked back to civilisation, making sure he was mostly dry before he was seen by anybody.

The townsfolk now knew him well, at least enough to wave as he passed by and offer a lukewarm, phlegmatic greeting. A few of the older gentlemen marvelled at his size and entreated him to take up boxing. Surprisingly, he made a mental note of that. It had the potential to bring in extra money, and he had some experience with it in his boarding school days. In fact, he missed the thrill, even if it had caused his nose to be broken so many times that he could not face forward for portraits anymore…

As he was dropping off a letter one afternoon, he caught the sight of a most peculiar figure he'd seen many times before.

Everybody knew of Albert Gillman, the magistrate's only nephew, and he was a beautiful fellow. He had a slim and streamlined silhouette, soft hair the colour of straw, and a pretty, youthful face, entirely smooth and unmarked by the creases of anger and worry, with well-formed lips always set in a relaxed pout.

Michael did not make the rules dictating what was and was not beautiful. He thought nature's best gifts were wasted on this marked being.

The peculiarity lied in his unusual manner. He often sat almost perfectly still on a stile, but his eyes seemed to drift around without purpose, and he could be found in that same spot when Michael walked to the post office and when he came back the other way. He'd locked eyes with him once or twice, and their look was vacant and unnerving, like a house that is fully lit, but nobody answers the door.

At first, he thought maybe he was blind, but he never seemed to have any difficulty getting around, and he had neither walking stick nor handler.

It was also common to find him running around with the local children, so Michael came to the conclusion that Albert was a bit…

Simple.

But as he didn't want to brave the impropriety of actually asking anybody, it remained an enigma.

On this day, Michael emerged from the post office and saw Mr. Gillman standing in an alleyway, directly across the street from him, with those eyes straight ahead, unresponsive to the people walking past. His heart leapt into his throat at the sight, but as he was not followed on his way back to the house, he decided the lad was harmless and shook the encounter from his mind with an involuntary shudder.

Wading through a herd of cats on his way up to the house let him know that Miss Alma had returned. He strolled round to the back and caught a glimpse of her gown streaming in the breeze. If he sauntered by ever so coolly, it would seem as though they crossed paths simply by chance.

She would probably not speak unless spoken to, so he frantically pieced together a topic of conversation.

A simple "good evening" would not suffice, and she has nothing he could offer to carry for her. It is almost too late. She is headed in the direction of the side door into the kitchen. If he goes in after her, it will appear as though he's following her (because he is).

"Going in so soon?" he inquired as he leaned against the wall and pointed out west. "And on such an attractive evening, with a sunset such as that?"

She paused and looked at the oppressively clouded purple sky. The sun was a rosy blotch, but heavenly beams of light still peeked from the crevices of the clouds as they moved away, so he did not feel like a complete moron.

"It is lovely," she mumbled.

"Yes it is," he folded his arms so that it would be less obvious that he was wiping sweat from his hands. "It'd be a pity, even a tragedy, to spend it indoors. Would it please you to walk with me, ma'am?"

She stared with that unreadable and searching expression, as if she did not know what to make of his words, and may have been trying to think of an excuse to decline. Now he was nervous, and was about to retract his offer, but she stepped away from the door.

"Alright."

She came up to him with her eyes darting every which way, occasionally fixing on him, but never for very long.

He waited. It seemed she was not going to lead the way, so he turned himself left, away from town, as he'd never gone that way before.

He turned back after ten or so paces when he did not find her beside him. She was about an arm's length behind and moving quite cautiously, but following sure enough, which is more than he'd expected. That awkward gait of hers made her hips sway and cling to her dress, especially walking up out of the steep ditch. It's not that he was specifically eyeing them, he just could not help but notice.

It really was a glorious evening, even with the extensive cloud coverage. The trees were beginning to blush red, and the dropping leaves swirled over the grass. Maybe one day he'd go out and climb high into those huge trees.

But his reason for venturing out was to get acquainted with this most interesting character. When she was not working, she was often shut up in her room, so he figured the best way to have a good word with her was to take her out of the house and away from her chores.

… perhaps he should have asked if she had any urgent matters to tend to before dragging her away.

"Ah, madam, you are not pressed for time, are you?" he stopped on the edge of the road.

"No, sir, not really," said she.

"Good, good. I'd hate to keep you from something important."

"Not at all."

They walked for some minutes' silence, but all the while, he inwardly fretted and cursed himself that he could think of nothing good to say. He paused for a little while, and a big and beautiful beetle meandered by his foot. Should he mention that to her? Maybe he should try and take it with him. Did she like beetles?

When he looked back at her, she did not seem troubled by this at all, even seemed peaceful and pensive. She gazed towards the emerging sunset with a tranquil but not rested expression, for her creased brow showed she was deep in thought. Now he did not want to disturb her.

It was maybe a mile from the doctor's home. Most of the houses spread out around them looked abandoned and quite decrepit. Weeds and briar overtook the blanched, dry woodwork, and the windows, if not boarded up, showed no signs of life.

"Isn't it sad?" Alma's voice just over his shoulder sent an odd shiver down his back. She was so small, he did not even see her when he turned his head.

"Isn't what sad?" he asked.

"Nobody is caring for those houses anymore. They're abandoned and we may not ever know why. It makes you wonder who lived there, why they're gone— what lives did they live? Who loved them? Does anybody even remember them? There's so much history trapped in those old walls."

There was a faint quiver in her voice, and such a distraught, passionate expression. These were thoughts that genuinely troubled her often.

He was completely still and rooted to his place, but her words imparted curious feelings upon him, and with those feelings, the urge to strain her to his breast.

"I suppose I never thought of it that way. Mainly, I was just thinking that after such a dry summer, they're one stray match away from going up in flames with this whole lot."

She emitted a strange, abrupt squeak that may have been stifled laughter. At least, he wanted to think it was.

She faced the sun as it touched the hills, now clear and radiant, casting a splash of colour over her, and her white face was the perfect canvas. The wind had changed directions. It blew the untamed strands of hair around her temples. He'd never taken notice of her hair until now; usually, it was pulled tight and neat, sometimes tucked into a hat. Now, it was loose and flowing, and he saw how summer had drawn out its brightness so that it shone like gold-wrought silk. The sight made him feel so warm…

"You've lived here your whole life, then, Alma?"

He bit his tongue. Why did he call her that aloud?

"Yes, sir, mostly," she was unfazed.

Michael was set at ease knowing she was not slighted. It was a difficult feeling, submitting to Dr. Webb and his family. The only man he'd ever answered to before that was his father. Even his tutors deferred to him.

"And you're quite attached to the place, I reckon?"

"I suppose so, though I've not travelled even north of London in many years. I think I should like to someday."

So she had her father's same wanderlust. That was the meaning behind her daydreams: she ached for a taste of adventure. She must feel like a caged bird, down here with no means to travel very far.

"Where would you go first? Say you have all the money in the world to spend."

Her features expanded and became quite gay.

"Well, I think I'd like to go to Africa! Many a people there have not been told the Good News we are charged with sharing!"

"Good News?"

"The Good News of our Saviour, of course!"

Our Saviour, she said. Michael had fancied himself his own saviour.

"And that is your first choice?"

"I see great necessity in it, sir."

"A most noble creature you are! Though I imagine you'd bake to death in that climate. You are unfit for labouring under a torrid sun."

"If I may, my brother and I both expected you to perish within a month here."

That bit him right where he was most tender.

"Most young women dream of going to Paris or Venice. I imagine that either one would be a much more fashionable retreat."

"You are coarse and unsentimental, sir."

"That, I may be."

Though he had tried to sound confident and worldly, he really seemed like a jackass when the words actually left his mouth. He decided that he wouldn't say any more.

Far east, everything was washed in blue, with shadows cast long across the land.

Michael looked over and saw Alma sheepishly roaming away from him, back to the house.

"Where are you going?"

"I'm cold, sir."

"Oh, yes— I do feel a bit of a chill, and God, you're in such a gauzy dress!"

"Are you staying out here?"

"I believe so, but wait a moment, A— Miss. Webb!"

"Sir?"

"We've known each other quite a while now, don't you think?"

"I suppose."

"And we've not even shook hands all this time!" he reached out to her. "Let us formally make each other's acquaintance."

Alma hesitated, with her hands clasped at her bosom, and slowly reached out her fingers for him to take.

Her hand disappeared into his, and it was so cold. She said she was, but it still surprised him.

"Will you take my coat, Alma?" Michael released her and began to disrobe.

"No thank you, sir, I don't need it," she was ambling away already.

"Your hands are ice! You'll catch death before you even get to the house! Take it, I insist."

She stopped and looked up at him, at the coat, and back at him.

Dammit, and stop looking at me in that way! he wanted to add.

She accepted it at last, but slipped it over her shoulders like a cape instead of wearing it normally. It swallowed her down to her knees.

Then she very subtly gave it a sniff, thinking he was not looking. That made him nervous. What did he smell like?

"Thank you, sir. Are you not cold yourself?"

"No, I don't get cold, Miss," he lied, thrusting his hands in his pockets so that they didn't tremble— though not from the cold.

To try to escort her back home may have been overstepping. There was no clear threat that he could see anyway, and he could see well with his hunter's eye. Besides, he wanted to enjoy every last bit of the waning twilight with this view.

Michael was so very pleased with himself. He could not feel the cold for the lingering warmth at his heart's core.

V

He found his coat hanging by the kitchen door when he came in the next morning. It smelled lightly of fresh cream, new blossoms, and old paper.

Breakfast was very light, only milk and a leftover rice pudding from yesterday's tea. Dr. Webb made it himself, and it was superb both hot and cold. Alma looked much more relaxed when she did not have to chase after her cousin or busy herself with cooking. He'd have asked why James did not cook more often, but he had already found that out the hard way.

Alas, Ida had actually been attending school lately, and had not graced them with her presence for quite a stretch. He enjoyed the tranquillity, though he was conditioned to hearing that rubber ball of hers bouncing through the hallway soon after he sat down. Alma was in the process of getting it through her head that dolls are for inside and balls are for outside, but it never seemed to stick.

Michael shared her uncle's suspicion that she delighted in being corrected, because attention was attention to such a demanding creature.

It must have been a lonely existence for her. He couldn't imagine that a lot of other children would play with somebody like her. He was quite isolated as a child, himself. Firstly, many children were intimidated by his social status, and secondly, he had a bad temper in his early puberty, and got into a lot of fights. He got along best with children a little older and a little younger; the former matched him in strength, and the latter liked that he could easily pick them up— especially the girls.

"Ah, Michael, I've been thinking," the doctor ran his finger along the rim of his coffee cup. He had been calling him by his Christian name as of late. "That old outhouse has kept you well thus far, but it's getting to be cold soon, and those walls may not be insulated enough to keep you warm through the night. It would be irresponsible to sleep with the stove running as well. So, if you'd like, we'll make up the spare room downstairs, and you can move your things in there starting tomorrow."

Now *that* was the *Good News!* He'd been in that little compartment for so long that he'd named all of the spiders. It would be a relief to finally move his belongings out of his trunks and into proper drawers, where they could be better organised. Moreover, his vanity had suffered greatly during his stay here. He could not hang his trousers up to stop them from creasing, and he did not have a good mirror or toilet spread to shave and make up his tie the way he liked to. He was only able to thoroughly wash and oil his hair once a week.

Moving his trunks inside was a task he undertook with great enthusiasm. His new room was as minimalistic as the majority of the house, with pristine whitewashed walls, a table next to the window, and a gorgeous set of brocade curtains, a most unexpected touch that he believed was reminiscent of home and served to renew his resolve. It was small, but not cramped, the ceiling was high enough that his hair did not brush against it. Best of all, the parlour was just around the corner, and he could read before bed without worrying about dropping books in the dirt (he said this to himself numerous times, but every time he grabbed a book, he always put it back unread, sometimes even unopened).

It was mid day, but he sprawled out onto the bed fully clothed and enjoyed all of that new space he had, and a delightfully smooth and firm mattress that he did not sink far into.

His room was directly across the hall from Alma's. He was acutely and consciously aware of this, and he held his breath when he heard her stirring within her chamber.

There was more work for him to do as the change in the season brought new demands. It was growing colder each day, and most of the cherries and wild blackberries picked in the summer were made into many jarred preserves, and those that were not sold were needing to be stored. They were fantastic on toast, even when it was fried in fat the way he liked.

That same afternoon, James Webb took Michael outside to point out his remaining tasks, starting with cutting up new wood.

And Miss Alma Webb was sitting at her bedroom window in one of her trances, combing her gilded hair. It was even more dazzling in the bright midday sun than dusky eventide, and it glittered as the breeze caught it. It fluttered as if it was lighter than air. If she were the princess Danaë up in her tower, then she produced her own shower of gold— to be one strand of that hair, touched so softly by those little white fingers…

"Bennett! Are you listening?" Mr. Webb demanded, now up close to his face.

"Ah— yes," Michael shook his head. "Cut up the hair— ahem, cut up the firewood and bring it to the house."

"And what else?"

"Um... I'm sorry— repeat it, please, old boy."

"You ninny!" he spat. "Take a decent portion of the wood to the church, and come back to clean out the cellar."

There was no rodent problem. Those cats were certainly earning their keep, but there were numerous occasions when he'd nearly stepped on them. As much as he abhorred them and their bawling, he didn't want to hurt them. He asked the doctor why there were so many feral cats but few dogs, and was told that cats were kept around for pest control, but dogs were often shot for fear of rabies. It pained him to learn that, but he did understand, and in some measure, he was glad, especially with all of the unattended children.

November was a very active month, and it began with another letter. Mail addressed to him? He both dreaded and anticipated it, hoping it had nothing to do with what he'd recently parted with...

Michael was maybe half correct. The name on the envelope set his blood on fire.

It was Abraham! He later learned that the old man had reached out to Dr. Webb months ago to

find out if he was there. This new letter was for
Michael himself, and so it read:

'Dear Master Bennett,

*It brings such joy to my withered old heart to
know that you are kept well! Every day I grieve
that we parted ways under such circumstances,
and have long suffered, as I feared for your
uncertain future.*

*All is well for me. I have found work in
Liverpool. I would much like for you to write
back to me yourself and tell me all you have
been up to, and how you will conduct yourself
moving forward.*

*I am ever grateful to Providence which protected
you, that you are safe, and I anticipate hearing
more of you.*

Abraham.'

Brief, yet so very poignant, as was his usual
nature. Not only did Michael prepare to write
him back right away, but he made note to ask Dr.
Webb for leave to visit him as soon as possible.
There was no chance in hell that he was going to
neglect the closest thing he had to family.

It would surely be a worthwhile investment to spend some of his savings on this trip. After all, one could not put a price on family.

That had been outlawed a long time ago.

The doctor did not object to a week's stay in Liverpool, and was elated that his correspondence with the butler had been successful. The date of his departure was set for November 23, just over two weeks from then.

In the meantime, he also did as much busywork as he could for people around town so that he could save up just a little more. Anticipation made him nimble.

The doctor usually went out when called upon, but patients often came to the house, as well. They were dispatched to the mostly empty room beside the parlour, and sometimes Michael was tasked with fetching things required for treatment. He had to learn a great deal of medical terminology very quickly, but thankfully, he was never involved in the procedures.

Ladies sometimes brought their babies, and he could hear them squealing. Cool and quiet Miss Webb eagerly fawned over them.

Michael did not have much experience with babies. He remembered once, when he was maybe twelve years old, that a piercing cry had lured him into a servant's room, and a scullery maid's unattended infant lay howling in bed. He called out, but nobody came quickly.

Unsure of what else to do, he carefully gathered it up and paced around the narrow chamber. He remembered that its sheer diminutiveness frightened him, for he could not believe that people could be so small, and he was dreadfully worried that he may somehow hurt it. Eventually, the wee thing's cries softened to whimpers, and that was when he should have put it down, but he stood and watched its little face and grasping hands, marvelling at this tiny creature, asking himself questions about existence that a child surely had no business pondering.

The baby was snatched from his hands, and he was flung out of the room by his shirt collar, scolded for wandering into a servant's private quarters— furthermore, such a large and ungraceful thing as he could easily crush it.

He remembered it any time he saw a baby. That type of memory stayed in your bones, not your brain. He felt it in his body when these little mothers visiting Dr. Webb regarded him with wary faces. How much more brutish he must have looked now, than at twelve…

And what could he do? Suppose he'd stood in the threshold as they departed, and stated, "I'm not dangerous!" It would not have been so humorous in practice.

When they looked at him in that way, he checked a scrap of paper in his pocket, and then his watch, as if he'd realised a task he'd forgotten, and left the house.

Three days before his departure, he was sweeping the pavement outside of the inn that evening, and it was not terribly crowded, so he could let his mind wander as he carried out the task. Unfortunately, it wandered off into places it was not supposed to, and he could not catch it in time.

Is this what you've been reduced to? A street sweeper? It asked.

I was not broken down, he answered it. *I chose this path for myself, and it is only temporary.*

That's what you think. You sink in the doldrums of this narrow life, and for a pitiful handful of breadcrumbs! For what? To live as a slave and die in your ancestors' home? How long do you intend to keep pretending? Cut your losses now

*and live as a free man on the continent,
employing yourself on your own terms.*

I am among friends, his own reply shocked him.
*I am content with this life if it means I am loved
by my fellow man.*

*These people are not your friends. They will
discard you once you are no longer useful to
them, and you surely know that. Why are you
really here? Is it an escape from your true
obligations as a man of status? This is an early
retirement, and retirement is far too dull for
someone like you.*

Michael stopped his ears, as if the voice was
external. He then continued sweeping like
clockwork, not thinking as he stepped back and
ploughed into some figure behind him.

"Oh! I'm dreadfully sorry—" he turned to
examine the sir or madam, and caught his breath
when he found his face inches away from Albert
Gillman.

The large, glassy eyes gaping back at him were
even more startled than he was.

"Sorry, sir—" he tried again.

But the Gillman fellow shuddered so violently
that his skeleton might rattle apart, and gave a

strange, hoarse cry before taking off and disappearing from the streetlights, into the sea of dusk.

He had never seen such an excitable man before, nor had he even seen Mr. Gillman out and about at this hour. It was like catching a ghost in its haunt. What was he doing out? He didn't seem to have a job.

As shaken as he was, he could not leave until he'd finished sweeping, but he turned his eyes every which way as he worked. Once he had done a thorough and acceptable job in his own mind, he retired the old straw broom and collected his payment.

"Took you a minute, there, lad," the store clerk noted.

"I tried to be as thorough as possible," Michael responded, and excused himself to return home.

Home… he was calling it home now…

For some strange reason, he could not shake off the feeling of those eyes following him on the way back.

Periodically, he turned, but there was no sign that he was being watched. Whatever wicked presentiment was upon him that evening, he was relieved to come inside, where it was warm, and his rifle was close at hand. By this time, his nose and bare hands were nearly numb. He hated gloves, because he could not feel what he touched, and he only wore hats when he absolutely had to. Abraham often upbraided him for this, as it made his complexion "uneven." His heart would give out if he saw him now.

It was now eight o'clock, and most of the lights were out already. A dim glow led him to the parlour.

Alma was at the table nearest to the hearth, with a stack of books before her. She had her attention fixated on just one of them and was scribbling in a pad. Her hair was loose, spilling into her chair, and she was in an old, flowing calico gown.

"What is that you're doing?" Michael took the liberty of warming his hands by her fire.

"I'm studying," as usual, she liked to keep an eye on what she was doing at all times. "I shall be attending training to be a nurse soon."

"A nurse? You?"

"Why not?"

"It seems you have your hands full as it is."

"Hardly so. I was growing tired of stagnation."

That made two of them, though as puzzling of a character as she was, he was not sure whether this surprised him or not.

"You like to work, then."

"I like stimulation. I never liked to be still for too long, be it physically or mentally."

"Do you ever feel sorry that you were born in such isolation, without much say in the world around you?"

She shrugged her shoulders, and then she wiped her glasses.

"We must cultivate our own garden."

That was the singular line Michael remembered from *Candide, ou l'Optimisme*. Of course, it was possibly the most iconic and regurgitated quote from Voltaire's writings, so he did not consider it a merit of her intellect.

Still, it was a charming answer in its own right, and quite like her.

Michael approached one of the empty chairs nearby.

"May I sit?"

"Be my guest."

He drew it close, perhaps a bit too close, and leaned forward to examine her work. She studied medical books, and he studied her. Her handwriting was proficient, if a bit inconsistent. Her sketches, though messy, were impressively detailed and accurate to the depicted diagrams.

Most notably, it seemed the firelight was her natural element. This ambiance suited her features the most, painting them in a highly contrasted but feathery-soft aura.

He was mesmerised by that flow of hair. In this light, it was gold and ebony. That calico gown exposed more of her chest and shoulders than her usual attire. Where the sun reached, her skin was creamy like ivory, but her shoulders were white as snow. Many would have found an uneven complexion to be unappealing, but to him, the white, untouched flesh was uncharted territory.

Her likeness, he imagined, was that of the fair folk; it could be fourteen or forty, completely apart from the human cycle of ageing, almost unearthly. The antiquated dress only enhanced the picture of timelessness. Her image could be captured in any century.

Yet her pale face was wrought so very red at this moment.

"Why are you flushed? What is the matter?"

"I am hot, sir, from stooping over this fire."

Alma stood up and straightened out her books and pencils, then pushed her glasses up the bridge of her nose with a dramatic flourish.

"Pardon me, I'd like to go have some water," she brushed past him, and the pressure left an impression on him somehow. He felt it even after she was long gone.

He watched the hearth. The fire had waned into a single lick against the grate. Looking at it made him sleepy, and he was plenty warm now, so he repaired to his room.

"I bid you goodnight, then, Miss Webb," he called into the kitchen as he passed.

Michael heard her light, unshod feet pass into the parlour again as soon after he'd shut his door. He pulled it ajar and leaned into the threshold. He listened long. It seemed they were the only two creatures astir in the house, even though it was not so late yet. Now he was not drowsy, not in the slightest.

He seemed to move on his own, back to the parlour, but not finding a lit fireplace, only a solitary lamp on the table. She was now reading from a bible.

A nurse, she said. That is what she wanted to be. A nurse was a tireless caretaker when you were sick or wounded, possibly even your companion in your final moments. He thought of this as he examined her, and remembered her continuous affection for that brat Ida and all those cats, her attentive and meticulous work ethic, and most of all, the great and consuming love within her that possessed her to desire a missionary life and fret over the fate of strangers long gone.

He knew what to call it now. And he was cruel for putting it down.

Michael came close and stood in front of her.

"Would you forgive me, Miss?"

She looked up from her book. He must have really engaged her at that moment.

"For what, sir? You have not wronged me. Though you are standing in my light."

He was.

"Oh, yes. I apologise."

"Then move."

She certainly was sharp when she wanted something. He did as he was told and took a seat across from her.

Did she really possess a servant's heart? He would put it to the test, or at least that's what he told himself he was doing.

"Would you read to me, madam?"

"Are you illiterate, sir?"

He should have expected her to be difficult when he encroached upon her quiet time with such a strange request, so he decided to be honest, even if it made him out to be a blockhead.

"To tell the truth, it's been a while since I really sat down and read, maybe even half a year's time. I've picked up a book, but I could never get past the first line before my eyes would crust over. Lord Bennett, my father, never pressured me to learn as yours does. If I perhaps had a good book read to me in such a soft and fine voice, I fancy I could get back into the habit."

The little drops of flattery seemed to roll off her back, but she consented.

"I will read from Ecclesiastes, because that is where I am compelled to read from, and so it must be essential at this time."

"Very well."

But she bent her head down and clasped her hands over the book, and her lips quivered.

After some time, he asked, "Miss Webb, are you alright?"

He had to wait a minute before she spoke.

"We must pray for discernment and wisdom each time we consult the Scripture, so that it might teach us new things."

"How many meanings can you get from one reading?"

"God's word lives and breathes, Mr. Bennett. It will speak to us continuously if we are inclined to listen."

Was she really a being from beyond the mortal world, that she spoke in this way?

"Do as you please, then, Miss."

"I did not know I needed your permission," she mumbled and opened to a marked place.

Alma read, and she seemed to have a habit of stretching her breath far beyond its limit, so that every other sentence had a warbling rasp towards the end, and then she would heave a great gasp. She stumbled over the words on occasion, and she wavered as she continued. Even so, it was a sweet voice, and those little quirks amused him.

He could vaguely recall the image of his mother when she read to him by candlelight. She had dark, shiny hair always arranged into a perfect part over her forehead, and her voice was heavenly smooth. She read until he dropped off to sleep, and sometimes she would curl up in his little bed with him.

Michael drew open the curtains. It was a marvellous, crystal clear night sky. A cat's eyes flashed in the distance and the creature darted away into the darkness. Only one half of the moon was lit, but the stars were dazzling. Sitting there between the warmth of the lamp and the cool starlight, he could almost imagine the world was a peaceful place.

"Mr. Bennett, you are not listening at all!" Alma's change in tone, though not severe, roused him from his stupor.

"Oh, pardon me," he sat up and rubbed his eyes.

"It seems you ought to *actually* be off to sleep this time, sir."

"Yes, you might be right," he pulled himself upright a little at a time. His neck creaked as he stretched out. "Then I will *actually* bid you goodnight this time, ma'am."

He reached out his hand. She took his fingers, but instead of a firm, hearty handshake, he got a weak grasp and prompt release. That would just have to sustain him.

"Goodnight, Mr. Bennett."

VI

The meaning of dreams, and if they even mean anything at all, has long been hotly debated by the scholarly, sceptical, and scriptural alike. Are they nonsensical blurs of residual unconscious thought? Are they a manifestation of our fears and desires? Or are they a premonition of things that shall soon come to pass?

Michael's preference depended solely on what kind of dream he'd had the night before.

On the night before his departure, he saw himself waking in the bedroom of his childhood, and for a moment he was seized by a burning joy, compelling him to leap from his bed and throw open the drapes. He may as well have been staring into a pot of ink. It was black and featureless outside, but he could see perfectly fine in his room, even though no light source could be found, nor could he make out faces in the pictures on the walls. There were never pictures on his walls.

Upon opening the door, he did not find the upstairs gallery, but remote, crumbling ruins like that which he beheld out in the fields. He heard a muffled, weak whimper somewhere. A cat? No, an infant. He looked around and saw no life. It grew louder and more anguished, and he tore apart the room in his search, turning furniture as easily as if it were paper, pawing at the floor in the darkness.

In a trunk, he found a baby that could not be older than half a year. Barbaric disregard for human life! Who would leave a child to rot in a trunk when a church would receive any foundling on its doorstep?

Michael retrieved the pitiful thing and exited the house, now finding, instead of his room, a steep, slippery crag jutting into the ocean. Its surface was smooth as glass, but he was assaulted with merciless wind and rain from all directions. The little child shrieked. He wrapped it up into his robe and ducked back inside.

When he turned around, he saw a woman seated at the far end of the room. Though the face was concealed, he immediately recognised that neat winged coiffure.

"Mammy!" he called out just as he did when he was a small boy. "There is a baby here, Mammy! Mammy, look!"

His mother did not answer him, and when he looked down at his arms, the baby was gone, and his fingers were warped and misshapen, dissolving like wet sand.

The roof had blown off of the house, and the walls collapsed, but he remained. Only a heap of lace and skirt was in his mother's place. No matter which direction he faced, he saw the facade of Ashwood Hall as a decrepit skeleton that he could never reach.

He was not awoken with a great start, but with a numb confusion and an ominous feeling about him.

The idea of breakfast was just not appealing to him that morning, but he agreed to take a piece of dry toast to appease Dr. Webb, the first person he found awake. He was usually one of the last to come out, but today he was early to send Michael off.

"Have you ever been to Liverpool, Michael?" he asked as he set water to boil on the stove.

"I have, sir. I've been to many cities, and I've been to Scotland and Ireland as well."

"Ah, Ireland is quite a beautiful land," the doctor sat himself down and lit his pipe, as he had exactly one smoke every morning when he first woke up. "I have in-laws from there, their mother's family," he waved his hand towards the hall, where James and Alma were presumably still asleep in their rooms.

"Your wife is from Ireland, sir?"

"Ah, no. But her parents are, and they settled in London nearly fifty years ago now. They had five children— five daughters— and she was their second."

"Did you like her parents, sir?"

"I've not seen much of them. Her mother has a quick temper, and was quite vexed with me for moving her into the country. I find that somewhat amusing, as my own mother fretted terribly when I left the country and briefly had a practice in the city! She swore the dirty London air would be my death, and wrote many letters imploring me to come home— up north, that is," he chuckled and idly gnawed on his pipe. "But I digress. Ellen, my wife, is estranged from her mother, and when I was first betrothed to her, she was ignorant of many things that I had to teach her myself, such as properly cleaning her teeth. That signifies neglect. Her hair was only down to her ears, as well; her mother kept it cropped very short as a child so that she didn't have to handle it. It took her many years to grow it out. Her father died when she was young, but to my understanding, he was not a good man at all."

"I see," it was well that Michael had declined a substantial meal that morning, because this alone was a lot to digest, and judging from the doctor's grave and disturbed expression, he did not want to ask what kind of man he had for a father-in-law. "Then is Mrs. Webb an equally unsavoury character?"

"Oh, no, my boy. We are merely different— far too different to live under one roof, and we get along best as we live now. For example, she likes fashion and finery almost in excess, and my tastes are practical. Meantime, we are equal in stubbornness and refusal to compromise. That besides, she is the mother of my children, my treasures. I could not speak ill of her."

Marriage was truly a daunting undertaking. Michael's parents had been blessed to be perfectly matched. His mother, Mary, was the niece of a textile magnate who, as an ailing bachelor, had made her his heiress, and his father was a young military officer: the second son of Lord Nathaniel Bennett. The arrangement was made so that Samuel would have a fortune, as his father was unwilling to split the estate. It was just as well that the two shared a love for animals, charity, and sports. The pair married at twenty-seven and twenty-four respectively, and she had courage enough to travel all across Europe and Asia with him before his brother died, and he claimed manor and title. Had Providence not found favour in them both, it could have been an unwanted fetter, a most unholy union.

"Do you think you should get married, Michael?" Dr. Webb broke his thoughtful silence.

That was a question he was not prepared to answer in great depth.

"Well, sir, I hardly think I'm prepared to maintain a thriving marriage at this time. As such, I think it best that I abstain from entertaining the idea for now."

Easier said than done.

"A fair answer. You are nineteen? I think folks are better off to wait until their twenties," he was pouring himself some coffee, and his eyes trailed away to behold Alma stepping into the kitchen.

"Papa, you didn't need to do all of that!" she huffed, referring to the brewed coffee and hot toast set out on the table. "If you'd woken me, I'd have gotten up and made breakfast!"

"Oh, it's no trouble, I think I can find my way around the kitchen well enough on my own," he poured more coffee and set it aside for her. "I'm not *completely* incompetent, you know. Sit down and eat, child."

The two lapsed into discussing her studies, and Michael was due to leave to catch his train. He stood and dusted himself off, and struggled to formulate a suitable goodbye to them both as he readied his luggage. He was travelling light. No aid was needed.

"I must be going," he first reached out a hand for Dr. Webb. That felt easier. "Farewell for now, sir, I'll be coming back soon. I'm sorry I could not stay to speak to James, but give him my best regards."

"Farewell to you, Mr. Bennett, until we meet again," the doctor stood and nearly crushed his hand and rent his arm from its socket. "I will oblige you, and you stay warm on your way to the station."

He turned to Alma. She was sitting motionless, staring at him, but very slowly held her hand out, without his prompting.

To his surprise, he was entirely calm and composed, but some unknown force possessed him to take that small, slight hand and brush his lips over the fingers.

"Farewell, Miss Webb."

"*Goodbye*," her reply was a barely audible whisper.

Michael went out the kitchen's outside door without another word.

"Where is he going, Papa?" he heard her ask as he descended the steps.

He walked on into town. It was plenty chilly, and there was a light drizzle picking up. He never disliked overcast, but he felt it was unfitting his restless anticipation.

On his way, he happened to cross paths with his most favourite person in the world, and he was alerted to her presence by the rock that bounced off of his shoulder.

"Had enough of this place, have you? Well good riddance!" Ida came skipping along in the opposite direction, with her hair done up in ribbons, and rocks in her gloved hands.

"Oh, I'll be back!" he turned on his heels as she passed. "And I'll have my revenge soon enough, just you wait!"

"Hah! You try anything and you'll be thrashed!" she readied more rocks to throw.

"Powerful words from somebody who's the perfect size for kicking!" he called back.

That was the end of that. The drizzle was becoming a shower, and he had to hurry.

This train ride was more tolerable than the last, as he was in better spirits during his trip. However, he had much more to think about, and more energy to think.

It seemed that Miss Alma Webb was not told he would be leaving, nor for how long. She looked so very distraught when he announced his departure, as well. Clearly it mattered to her whether he was around or not, then, yes? Was he arrogant for seeing significance? After all, she has shown herself to be a caring and compassionate person. How would she receive him when he returned? Now, more importantly, what did that mean to him, or for him?

VII

Michael set foot in Liverpool that afternoon, and this time, he made sure he knew the address well. He decided he would do well to get a professional shave and trim before he arrived, and then he made his way to the dignified townhouse where his old friend resided.

He knocked, and he waited.

The door opened, and Michael was greeted with a familiar face he'd long missed.

"Bless me! You came!" Abraham had clung to him and was kissing him before he'd even stepped inside.

"Of course I did! I said I would!"

"Ah, come in, come in!" he was already taking his hat and suitcase from him, as if he was still the butler. "I'll make you some tea! I remember just how you like it!"

"Please don't wait on me, Abraham! I'm here as a friend, after all!" he tried to paw at his suitcase, but the old man continued as if he'd not heard him.

"Nonsense, you're a guest, and I shall treat you thus!" Abraham waved off his concerns.

Michael thought the spread of the city outside was pristine, but Abraham's parlour was positively spotless. Everything but the floor was snowy white, save for just a touch of yellow in the wallpaper. Even the woodwork was whitewashed. The seats and couches were covered in cloth. Not a speck of dust could hide in that room. It was quite fitting for the man who always scolded him for touching the paintings and armour pieces, and sitting on the carpet.

"My, you keep a good house!" he marvelled as he sat down. "Do you share it with anybody?"

"I don't, sir," Abraham replied as he served tea, and sliced rolls of bread. "I do like my privacy, but it's a joy to see you again! I was so very thankful just to hear from you, but to have you here is a gift from God!"

"And what do you do for work here, Abraham?"

"Oh, I am a driver for some of the affluent, pretty people here. It was easy to obtain with my credentials, and it pays well enough. The good doctor has you working for him, you say? Running errands? What do you make from him?"

"Thirty-five shillings a week."

Abraham's mild, drooping eyes widened. "My, that's money! He really has set you up nicely!"

"... it is?"

"Oh yes, anybody doing such an easy job would be grateful for that pay! There's many a body not far from here that toils all the daylight hours and can barely afford a sack of flour each week!"

Michael remembered how he'd bemoaned his pitiful wages, and he felt himself blush. He would meditate on this quite often later, but for now he had things to take care of.

"Could you refer me to a nice inn for my stay? I imagine I'll turn in very soon."

"An inn? Oh, nonsense! You'll stay here, I've plenty of room, even for a fellow as big as you!"

"No, no, Abraham, I wouldn't impose my presence upon you!"

"Nonsense!" he said once more. "I just finished telling you how it eases my old heart to have you as a guest, and you spurn my hospitality! Humour me for just one week!"

It occurred to Michael, just then, that as Abraham was nearly ninety, and a life-long bachelor at that, he possibly had no family left, or at least none that would claim him. For decades, the Bennett family had been his whole life.

Well, he could not refuse a plea such as that. He consented to take up temporary residence in Abraham's guest chamber. With all of the affairs settled for the time being, they could simply catch up and reminisce about simpler times.

Still, money continued to be a topic of discussion.

"Surely your father's debts were not so staggering that even selling that vast estate left you with nothing to your name," Abraham pulled at his fingers, a nervous tic of his.

"No, I've roughly seven thousand pounds in the bank."

"Goodness me! And you've not touched it all this time?"

"I've tried not to. You see… I've been meaning to one day buy the estate back."

"Ah, Master Bennett," he still called him that. "Are you sure you will? I fear that could take an entire lifetime of savings at your pay rate, and I daresay you're not skilled in many trades. Do you not think you should use those funds for your education?"

"I must buy it back, Abraham. I may have cancelled the debts owed by my father, but now I owe a personal debt— a spiritual debt: to myself and my ancestors."

"Oh, I've always fretted over the decisions your father made…" he pulled his fingers some more. "He would not send you to college, local or abroad, nor would he pressure you to take up any valuable skills. After your mother and sister died, he became reckless to keep you completely attached to him, and I feared it was at the detriment of your growth. He indulged your love of sport, but he would not push you even in that sphere! Oh, I tried to talk some sense into him, but he'd not have it… he failed you…"

These words struck him, and if any other man on Earth had uttered them, Michael may have started swinging, but he could only sit there and blink the venomous sting from his eyes.

Abraham saw that he ached, and dropped balm where his words cut.

"Master Bennett, your father loved you. That much is more certain than anything else in the world, and I could never deny that. Moreover, I think that the makings of a good man are at work within you. You have handled your hardships with more grace than many in your position likely would. But please reconsider, for your own sake: live for your own happiness, and be content with what you've been given. You are much too young and too full of potential to waste your life."

"I'm sorry, Abraham. I've made up my mind."

"Compromise! Graduate and become a skilled and prosperous man, and buy your homeland with superior earnings."

"I'm close, Abraham. I have about half of the funds I need as it is."

He abandoned the finger pulling and now furiously rubbed his brow.

"Lord, oh Lord… the Bennetts have always been a stubborn breed. Well, Master Bennett, your fate is in your hands as much as it is in God's, and I will pray over your safety as I always have."

"The sentiment is appreciated, old friend, but don't worry about me."

Abraham continued to worry. He did not voice his concerns, but it was always etched on his weathered brow. Regardless, he remained as cordial and courteous as he had always been, save for his impatience when it came to clutter.

Of course, Abraham could not take leave from his job. Each day, he offered to drive Michael around anywhere he wanted free of charge, just in case he'd missed the experience.

As he had not visited this beautiful city in nearly a year by now, Michael took him up on that offer many times during his trip, and even wore gloves and a hat just to please him. When he'd been dropped off, he would then walk by himself in the lovely and wealthy sect, dressed in one of his best suits, with his watch chain glittering from his pocket. He expected to blend right in, but to his surprise, he felt a measure of displacement and discomfort that he could not understand. The elegant and sophisticated conversations he thought he'd participated in during his youth now sounded low and dull, only dressed up with pedigreed accents and flourishing gestures.

Under the powder, gems, and false fringe, the wealthy ladies of Liverpool looked just the same as the low-born women of the country. The young girls did not blush under their veils when he greeted them, if they even looked his way.

The most attention he'd gotten was when a smiling, pretty red-haired lass with shining teeth asked him how much he was worth, and she nearly swooned (or wanted him to think she did) when she interpreted seven thousand pounds as an annual salary, and he did not bother to correct her.

What had changed since he had abandoned this life?

"Are you pleased to be back in your element for the time being, Master Bennett?" Abraham asked one morning after breakfast before he set out.

"You need not call me that, Abraham," Michael was still fastening his watch, and putting on his coat. "My title is empty, as I own nothing, and I am the master of nobody except myself— hardly even that."

The reply he received was a peculiar one:

"My loyalty is not to the title, nor the money, but to the Bennett family. Even if they no longer pay me, they will always have mastery over me in some way."

"Well, if it would please you, you may continue to call me whatever you wish. But to answer your question, I do suppose I quite like it."

He set aside time to dine at one of the finest restaurants in the city, and of course, he brought Abraham with him and was glad to treat him to any dish he wanted. After much hushed bickering, he was convinced to order what he truly craved, not what was the least expensive. Michael finally had his prized mulled wine, which was every bit as marvellous as he remembered, stirring up memories as sweet and piquant as the hot beverage. At least that one thing had not changed.

His days were refreshing and stimulating, but his nights were often troublesome. The same image kept invading his dreams, of the infant locked in that wooden trunk, but even when he tried to tear off the rusty lock with his bare hands, it would not budge, and the awful shrieks and howling winds grew louder as he became frantic.

Even though he would have most definitely been strong enough, he could not try to break open the trunk, for fear that he would harm the child. He thought for a moment that he should cry out for help, but who was there to help him? He sobbed, growing sick from effort and desperation as those cries started to fade away, and the ruined house spilled over the edge of the cliffs. He always awoke just before they were both crushed.

These were the dreams that shook him from his slumber in a feverish sweat, but he kept them to himself, as he did not want to burden Abraham's tender heart with such awful imagery.

So, for the first time in his life, he wrote them down. If he could intimate his thoughts to even an inanimate object, then he would not have to be tortured by them. He started by writing just his dreams, soon after waking up so that he did not forget. It felt as though a weight was being lifted.

He did not stop there. The words came naturally. Soon, he was writing about his plans for the future, and of course, the people he'd met along the way: exactly how he felt about them as if he had to describe them to somebody. It was almost a challenge. Maybe by doing it on paper, it would become easier to do so aloud. He was never good at explaining his feelings to or for other people, but he did his best:

'Abraham, the old butler, is a trusted and faithful friend that never has an unkind word to say; just as lively at eighty-six as he must have been at twenty. He is as dear to me as a grandfather, and I love him with my whole heart.'

It was not difficult to write his true feelings for the old man. He had been a constant presence for his entire life, and even knowing he was in the next room made him feel secure.

'Dr. Henry Titus Webb is something of an uncle to me. He has given me so much more than I even realised at first, and I owe him beyond measure.'

Finally, he could truly articulate his gratitude to those two fine men. It made him feel warm.

'Ida Clarke is... a child. I am not particularly fond of children, and she has done nothing to change my mind.'

Wait… that wasn't true. He never had any issue with children. Ida had poisoned his mind. No surprises there. She surely knew good and well that he could not stand her, and she may have even prided herself on it.

'Bratty children,' he corrected himself in the margins.

'Albert Gillman is a strange fellow that stays at a distance, and I prefer to keep it that way. He makes me uneasy. Pardon the barbarism in the description, but despite his handsome and unobtrusive face, or even because of it, I find him wholly abhorrent and think him quite simple. Judging by his look, I imagine he has handlers just to dress him in the morning.'

That piece was especially cathartic, and since he doubted anybody noteworthy would read these passages, he did not hold back the wicked emotions astir within him. He burned with an evil passion as he vented what he repressed.

'James Webb is alright, just alright. He is fine to work with, and though our tastes and manners differ, I find him mostly personable.'

James was a man of few words, and something of a recluse. Michael did not have many strong feelings for him one way or the other, and the sentiment seemed to be mutual. Writing about him was no chore, except maybe to find enough to say.

'The innkeeper Mr. Briggs is charming, if curt. I am sorry for grumbling about his tavern's limited stock when I first arrived. He is a hard-working man running an honest business, and the cider he serves is quite good.'

As for Alma, he saved her for last, and his pen froze over the paper when he tried to get it over with.

'Get it over with?' Michael scolded himself. *'Don't treat it with such indignation!'*

He looked down and realised he had really written that down. He grabbed a clean sheet.

After some minutes of staring at the stark white page, he penned his first attempt:

'Miss Alma Webb is an interesting character...'

That was the truth, but it was not the whole truth.

'Her mind tends to wander it seems, though not to the extent of Albert Gillman—'

Michael furiously scratched out that line. Miss Alma and the Gillman did not belong in the same sentence. The clear, sharp eyes that shone like real gems did not compare to those glassy, dim, almost bulging lamps. He even felt a degree of shame and disgust that he had put the two of them together.

'She can be quite slippery and elusive, even sardonic at times.'

He did not scribble out that sentence, because it was partially true. She could indeed deliver a piquant and well-timed remark, but he had to share some of that responsibility. He often provoked her with his eccentricities, and he was aware of that, but sometimes he could not help it. The reactions and peculiar little smiles tickled him.

Still, he was not being completely honest. Why was it so difficult?

'She has a strong work ethic, and is very charitable, and though she is a dreamer, she has a good head on her shoulders...'

He was getting close, he could feel it, but he was still beating around the bush. His heart began to pound so fast and hard against his ribcage that it rustled his shirts. The words poured freely:

'She is such a noble figure, and her heart is so pure and tender. She has been far more kind and courteous to me than anyone should ask of her, and certainly more so than I would deserve. Her bright and brilliant mind is too good for the existence she submits to. It would delight me to offer her so much more. I wish she would ask me for anything at all, even command me. I want to yield to her. Why does my heart beat faster than I can measure as I write this?'

His penmanship suffered under his trembling hands. The pen was now too slippery to properly grasp. The letters were misshapen, and peppered with wet blots and smears. It now seemed improper to confide in a thoughtless leaf of paper.

When the ink had dried, he tore out the paragraph and slipped it into his breast pocket. It felt heavy and hot. The impression of that passage was engraved on the paper underneath it. Now, he went back to sleep, as it was still dark out.

He was thoroughly fatigued, and his nerves frayed, but there was satisfaction in the feeling. This, he believed to be a much more strenuous exercise than swinging a scythe and chopping firewood.

VIII

On that last day of his visit, Michael was packing his suitcase and then standing to one side as Abraham showed him how to do so "correctly," when he was presented with the most fateful decision he'd have to make since this journey began.

"Master Bennett," Abraham shut up and corded his luggage, staring down at his feet with a heavy, weary look. "I meant to tell you this on the day you arrived… "

He sat down, so Michael seated himself as well, and leaned in to listen to him.

"Your father set me up with a hefty sum of money that I would be granted upon his death. He insisted, though I told him I shan't be needing it. I still do not believe that I need it, as I do fairly well for myself here…"

Michael waited, and Abraham began to tug his fingers again, then he saw him produce a chequebook and scribble into it.

"I have two thousand pounds that I've not touched, Master Bennett. Take it— take it, please."

Michael swallowed down his nerves. That would put him at nearly nine thousand pounds. That was close, so close…

"I cannot accept that from you, Abraham."

His expression became taut and anguished.

"Master Bennett, please understand: I knew of the debt your father was in, and I stayed quiet… you know, he became agitated so easily in those final days… but I have committed an awful treachery against you by my concealment— oh, if only I had talked him into selling the estate himself— it was inevitable. Instead, it fell squarely on your shoulders!" his face waxed deep red and his eyes welled up.

He drew a long breath to steady himself before he finished.

"So take it, Master Bennett. Take it so that I might make it right."

With that amount, he could hope to purchase the estate back in maybe fifteen or twenty years. He would still be reasonably young.

Close… so close…

Michael yearned and ached to accept it. It called to him. He panted with the effort of restraint, and itched with desire.

"Abraham," he sighed. "That money is rightfully yours. You have been a loyal servant to the family for longer than I've even lived. It is the least you deserve."

"Master Bennett—"

"If you will still call me 'Master,' then I will act as such; *keep it*, Abraham, I command you!"

Michael cringed at exploiting rank when it was currently meaningless, but appealing to authority was the only way to get through to him.

"Very well, sir," he resigned and placed his book back into his coat.

"It is very well, indeed, Abraham, old boy," he clasped his shoulders in his hands. "You are truly among the most stalwart of men, and I thank you for your service."

"Bless you, sir," the butler choked out as he began to sob.

"My, how sensitive you are!" Michael teased as he kissed that wrinkled cheek and dashed away the tears with his shirt sleeve. "I forgot a temperament such as yours should be handled with care!"

As for him, he spent the rest of that day battling the terrible nausea that plagued him soon after.

Abraham elected to drive Michael to the train station himself. This parting was not so solemn and bitter, as there was certainty in their promises to meet again.

"Please continue to write me, boy," Abraham held onto his free hand all the way to the steps. "And come see me any time, I won't be going anywhere anytime soon, unless this shrivelled old body gives out!"

"*Pish!* You'll outlive me, I'm sure of it!"

"Nonsense!" he sent him up the steps with an affectionate shove. "You're sturdy as an oak tree already! And by the bye I'm proud of the gentleman you've grown into, and I'm sure Samuel would be too, Michael."

Abraham had never called him by that name before, never in his life. It would have been uncouth and unacceptable under any other circumstances, but Michael welcomed it. He took his seat as the doors closed, and looked out the window for one more glimpse of an old friend.

He was far off, waving his hat over his head, but when Michael squinted hard, he saw a look of apprehension and distress.

It was near dusk when he arrived, and the stars were out by the time he reached the stile. He'd not been gone for long, but it felt like an eternity since he'd seen those shutters. There were low lights inside.

Dr. Henry Webb was sitting on the porch, smoking a cigar instead of a pipe.

"Hallo there!" Dr. Webb saw him scaling the stile and beckoned him forward. "Get up here and out of the cold!"

He advanced, and the doctor looked him up and down.

"Look at *Lord* Michael Bennett, coming up the street like an ordinary fellow, leaving his butler behind and carrying his own luggage— set that down, then, I'll bring it in for you."

He flicked a stub of ashes into the grass, and continued chattering away as they stepped inside.

"You are late! I thought you would never arrive today, and I would have to pawn all of this rubbish in my guest room! Probably make a pretty penny, too."

"It is nice to see you, sir," Michael took off his hat and muffler in the hall.

"Yes, welcome back, son. I know you've travelled a long way, so I won't keep you. There is a good fire in the parlour; go on ahead of me and get warmed up. I have work to do upstairs."

Michael held up a little burlap bag he'd brought with him: "I have oranges for everyone, sir."

"Oh! We don't get fresh oranges here very often. Alma will be very pleased."

Even the cool and brooding James Webb rose up to shake his hand when he entered. Alma did not stand to greet him, as she had a fat calico cat in her lap to match her calico dress. She only stayed put and stroked it while it squirmed, roused by his arrival.

"Sit down," she offered with her head bent down.

He took the cautious liberty of sitting beside her on the couch.

"It is a pleasure to see you again as well— and look at the size of that fat thing!" Michael exclaimed incredulously as it hid its face and dozed contently in the plentiful folds of fabric. "One of Ida's little balloons?"

"This is Sophie, sir," Alma's quivering voice betrayed her attempt at a stiff upper lip. "She will soon have kittens. I've brought her inside to separate her from the rest and to keep her warm."

"Oh, thank heavens, more cats."

"She is a docile one, sir. She is used to people and would not give you any trouble."

"It will be trouble enough when everything in the house is covered with fur."

"You needn't complain so much when you're not even the one who will clean it up."

"Perhaps I complain on your behalf."

"What a kind soul you are."

"If I see it in my room I'll stick it with a needle and pop it."

James and Alma lapsed into fits of laughter at his absurd statement, much to the dismay of Sophie.

"That would be a waste!" James gasped. "I think it would roll quite well if you kicked it down the hill!"

Alma still laughed, but she protectively drew the cat close, as if her maternal feelings had been injured by this nonsensical banter. It purred loudly enough for Michael to hear, and curled up against her bosom.

What callous misjudgment had come over half of him, that he could denounce these people? These were true friends, or at least he thought they were, and he was pleased to be in their presence again, even if it meant tolerating the cat.

James got up and left the parlour, and Michael both blessed and cursed him for doing so. Now he was alone with Alma… and the cat.

Not only was he alone with her, but he was *beside her,* and close enough to feel her heat and hear her breath. The paper he'd torn was still in his pocket.

"Miss Alma, are we friends?"

"I would say so, sir."

"And you had not forgotten me entirely, and replaced me with this swollen tick?"

"I should think not, sir, as the two of you do not compare. She is soft to touch, easy to please, and does not make much noise."

He scoffed and huffed, "I see you are as biting as ever before."

She did not reply, only kept caressing the cat as if she had not heard him.

Michael remembered, at that moment, when he compared the women of the country to the refined ladies of gentry, and found them to be equal. And what was Alma?

By law, she was not ugly, nor was she a conventional strapper; she had a bit of colour about the hands and neck, but elsewhere, she was a little too pale. She was shapely but not tall and buxom, her eyes were fierce instead of passive, and her feet were too large for her stature, though her hands were slight, slim, and soft. Upon close inspection, there was a light dusting of freckles on the whole face… even on her mouth… on her chest…

Yet he could not even rightfully say she was plain or average, because all of these, though not handsome by convention, moulded a most unique little figure that he could not help but be drawn to, and they accentuated each other with their contrasts. For example, the pale face blushed a deeper red than most, and the sharp, engaging eyes, large forehead, and prominent cheekbones were balanced by the rounded, delicate chin and little rosebud lips.

Such a jewel was disguised, or maybe intensified by the subdued dress and peculiar manner. It did not even seem fair to judge these elfish features based on the standards of man.

In short, she was beautiful.

He always knew that, but now, he was ready to admit it to himself.

Though… the old calico dress still fascinated him: a young lady in such an outdated article, possibly older than her parents, when she has means enough to possess a few fashionable pieces. He knew she had at least one. He'd seen her smart modern church dress before.

"Anyway… what do you wear this set of rags for?" He pinched a bit of sleeve between his fingers. The contact gave her a strange little shuddering start, and he let go.

"It was given to me. My aunt found it in her house when she moved in thirty years ago, in an old trunk that she imagined had not been touched in ages. She adored it for its full skirt and gentle pattern, but it was too small for her, and she thought it would just be a sin to cut up such a sweet relic, so she let me have it. She did not mind parting with it because it pleases her to know it is in loving hands."

"Will you ever adapt it to modern tastes?"

Her face contorted into a look of shock and even disgust.

"I would not dream of it, sir! This gown has been cared for in this shape for decades, and some woman must have loved it well. When I think of it, it's something my grandmother may have worn, and I like it just the way it is."

"Precisely the response I'd expect from you," he attempted to stroke the abhorrent creature in her lap. His fingers were not covered in filth, itch, and boils when he returned it, so it was probably alright. He was still going to wash his hands.

"I see you've overcome your feline fear!" Dr. Webb had entered the parlour as silently as his daughter might have tread.

Of course this comment stabbed Michael right in his manhood— but he pardoned himself for feeling slighted, as things that are so new and young are often tender.

"I find them to be unnecessary creatures, sir. We already have foxes, weasels, and snakes that eat rodents."

"How can a *weasel* be better than a cat?" Alma curled her lip and leaned into the arm of the couch.

"They don't shed nearly as much, and they stay away from people."

"They are loud and wasteful."

"Are you not fond of animals, Michael?" Dr. Webb took a seat where James sat before, surprisingly not holding his pipe. The cigar must have satiated his tobacco cravings for the night.

"I am indeed, sir!" he replied sharply, as if his honour had been challenged by the question. The truth was merely that he had never gotten along with cats, and found them a burden on the environment. "I particularly enjoy horses and dogs. I've had both, and they do make faithful company."

"He doesn't enjoy the chickens, though," Alma added.

"It's mutual. The chickens don't enjoy me, either."

"Ah! A pity you weren't here before our old mare Betty passed away two years ago— Alma was deathly afraid of her when she was little! Mrs. Webb took the goat, and that's why the barn has only cats and chickens now."

"A pity indeed," Michael had not gotten to ride a horse in so long. He missed feeling like a giant among men with his great grandfather's garrick coat streaming in the wind. He'd brought it with him…

Alma stood up and placed Sophie on the floor.

"Goodnight, Papa; Mr. Bennett."

"Goodnight, Alma, my good girl," the doctor bowed his head.

She left without waiting for Michael to acknowledge her. The cat waddled after her sweeping skirt, with its big belly swaying.

"She is a hard-working little lady, I tell you," Dr. Webb mused when they heard her door shut. "In addition to her studies, her house work, and occasionally assisting at the pharmacy, she herself insisted upon nursing that mama cat she has with her."

"I think it is admirable, sir," Michael admitted, and he believed it to be the truth.

"It is so. Any man would find in her a diligent wife, that is certain, and she is plenty affectionate when she wants to be. She's not selected an ideal suitor, though."

"Does she have suitors, sir?"

"Oh, yes. Mrs. Webb, her mother, has set up many appointments for her to meet and choose her intended husband."

That was a blow, but Michael was sitting down, and was in no danger of fainting or staggering.

"Will she be getting married soon, sir?"

"She will do as she pleases. I doubt she wants to be married in the immediate future. Though, I think it is too early for her to be married anyway, and as she is not yet twenty and living in my house, I have the authority to send away any suitor I deem unfit."

It was a lot to take in, but he processed it as well as he could. He thought of it as he got himself ready for bed, as well, and the next morning as he bathed his flustered face after a fitful night's sleep.

Though he felt sick with many confusing feelings, he was ravenous from skipping dinner yesterday, and was more eager to rise for breakfast than he ever was before.

Alma seemed very pleased to see him clean his plate and ask for another heap. It always satisfied her to see people enjoy her cooking, and he sorely missed it himself. She'd risen early and prepared an abundance of eggs, salt pork, potatoes thinly sliced and fried crisp, and toast the way he liked it.

Dr. Webb, on the other hand, was pleased to see him clean his plate because a hearty breakfast would "stick to your ribs," and he was, indeed, going to be put back to work that very day, working outside in the cold.

There was no shortage of fatty trimmings left over, and Sophie the cat ate to her heart's content. Even Michael offered her scraps to eat from his hand, and she paid it back with licking and purring. He tolerated it, then he stood up to dress himself for the day.

If he was being honest, it felt wonderful to get back to work, because it was something he was actually good at.

Cutting up firewood was easy and had a mesmerising rhythm to it, especially with a good axe. He sometimes fell into the clockwork routine and continued to work more than was required of him. While he worked, he did not even mind the chill, though it was now early December and growing bitterly cold. Hauling the wood where it needed to go was easiest of all, and he loved walking in any weather.

Fortifying the barn, specifically the chicken enclosure, was not so enticing. It required a precision that he was unsure of, and much more concentration for that reason. On top of that, the chickens were quite obnoxious, and he'd never gotten along with them.

"Afternoon, ladies," he approached them slowly so that they did not make a scene and made sure they were distracted with plenty of feed. Even so, it made him uneasy to be alone with them, and he was always looking over his shoulder as he worked.

He started by removing planks that were starting to rot and come apart. That was easy. If the nails were still good, he reused them. James supervised him for maybe thirty minutes before deciding he could fend for himself.

The cold really started to bite as the sun sank down and the wind picked up. He could ignore it as long as he did not stop moving for too long.

The task was a bit less intimidating once he'd gotten used to it, and the chickens were too lethargic to bother him. He kept at it until deep into the afternoon, when there was not much sunlight left.

"Mr. Bennett, that's enough for now!" Alma's voice was a silver bell over the whistling wind. "Come inside and eat!"

It wasn't finished. Everybody had habits and inclinations that they took to almost compulsively; Abraham had his affinity for neatness, Miss Webb always dried the rim of her cup before she set it down, and Michael could not leave a task unfinished. Doing so made him itch and pine, and he could focus on nothing else.

Still, her voice drew him towards the house.

Once he'd set down the tools and retired from his labour, he realised just how cold, hungry, and sore he was. Alma standing in the doorway to the kitchen was an angel calling him to the gates of heaven.

The damp chill in the air had numbed his ears and nose. His legs were two stone pillars he had to drag up the steps, but he made it to the threshold alive and on his feet. She had a very simple repast of warm brown bread and butter, sliced cheese, and hot coffee set out waiting for him.

He hated coffee.

"Madam, I thank you for the sustenance after a long day out in that merciless cold," he held his inflamed hands over the steam from the kettle. "But do you have anything other than coffee for me to drink?"

"We are out of tea, sir. Drink the coffee or continue to shiver."

Well, if it would warm his bones a little faster, he would suffer through the pungent, almost rancid bitterness.

Michael poured a mug for himself and smelled it first. The scent was deceptively enticing. He took the smallest, most pitiful sip and scrubbed the taste out of his mouth with a crust of bread. The effort of choking it down made him shudder and pinch up his face, meanwhile Alma sipped a long draught from her cup with pleasure. How did she drink this without even any milk? Good bread was being wasted to bind with this poison.

"Have you any milk or sugar?"

She saw his distaste, and a wicked glint flashed in her eyes.

"Shall I also cut the crust off of your bread so that you can swallow it?"

"Miss, if you think I'm just going to sit here and let you bully me," he took another drink; disgusting. "You're absolutely right."

She still brought out a little pitcher of milk and spooned some into his coffee. That made it a bit smoother going down, at least. He finished it as quickly as he could so that he could enjoy his meal. Now he was hot and flushed, and his body wanted to reject it.

They ate quietly, and he could not stop himself from thinking of what he'd been told last night. When he'd studied Alma's face that day, she did not seem to be troubled or in a great hurry; she was even relaxed. She was eating bread and butter with bits of peeled orange, gazing peacefully out the window. He felt compelled to ask her about it himself, but the words caught in his throat when he tried to speak, as if even his own body knew he should not dare to enquire.

"Alma," he croaked out and reached towards her, and she recoiled at the sight of his cracked and bruised fingers.

"Goodness!" She snatched his hand and brought it up to the light to examine it, and he smelled the orange perfuming her fingers. The touch smarted, yet it sent a thrill up his arm. "I didn't realise your hands were blistered! Where are your gloves?"

"I don't like gloves," he answered.

"Wait here, and I'll get a salve for them," she disappeared into the hall, apparently too alarmed to even scold him.

That spared him the embarrassment of enquiring about affairs that were none of his business. He was meant to be proud and bold; all the Bennetts were. But when it came to Alma, he found himself wavering.

The cat was sleeping on a bundle of straw and rags in the hall. It perked up and followed Alma as she passed, its plume of a tail disappearing into the shadows.

"I think Papa will be home late today," Alma returned with a cat at her heels and an old tobacco tin full of a mysterious jelly. "But when he gets back, you should tell him to give you work that's gentle on your hands tomorrow— my, they're raw!"

"They sting a bit," he admitted, as coming from the cold outdoors into this heat had made them burning hot, and taut as new leather.

"You should have come in when they started to ache, at least to warm them up a little."

Alma used a damp cloth to sponge the slime onto his hand, starting with the left, the useless one. It smelled strongly of menthol and alcohol, and it was like being stuck with hundreds of little pins for only a moment before it brought cooling relief.

Just as he tried to reach for more bread and cheese from the plate, she'd seized his right hand.

"Miss Alma, I'm still hungry, and this balm, though fragrant, would not make a good condiment."

She responded by folding it into a little sandwich with her clean hand and bringing it right up to his face. It took him entirely too long for him to realise he was supposed to eat it (just as it had taken him too long to realise a lot of other things).

Michael thought he was going to float away. Between the coffee and close contact making his heart race, and the soothing, intoxicating aromas, he was lighter than air.

He knew it was only her nature to tend to him, just the same as she would look after an injured sparrow long into the night, and yet he could not help but feel so very warm and special. The way she softly hummed and mumbled to herself as she worked was too precious to put into words. He wanted to gather her to his breast and have her all to himself.

Alas, as long as the cat was purring and butting its head against her legs, he had to share her attention.

"You're such a pretty kitty," she crooned as she patted its bulbous flank and set a saucer of milk down for it. "You'll have the most beautiful babies, won't you?"

Beautiful babies, indeed. Kittens in their first weeks of life more resembled rats than cats.

"And this will heal my hands, yes?" he folded them on the table in front of him, now that they weren't so tender. They tingled from the menthol, but it was a pleasant sensation.

"Oh, this jelly will fix just about anything as long as you keep it on for a while. I made it myself, and it's even a part of my beauty regimen," Alma shut the tin and gathered up the supplies she'd brought to the kitchen.

"Will it make me pretty?"

"That is beyond the power of any elixir, sir, but with what's in it, I imagine it may lighten these stubborn freckles on my face."

"Why would you want to do something like that?" He demanded, unfazed by the insult to his own looks (he was no flower, he always knew that), but amazed at the prospect of removing those peculiar little spots.

"They make the complexion uneven," she cast a sideways glance his way, as if he had said something thoughtless and absurd.

Maybe he had, but now he was quite impassioned and could not be stopped, because he believed in his own words.

"They make it interesting. Nobody has them in the exact same arrangement, but a clear and spotless face does not stand out— a clear face is charming in its own right, don't misunderstand me— but it lacks singularity. Such characteristics make the wearer stand out in ways they may not otherwise… well, I'm not saying you wouldn't have stood out anyway…"

His voice trailed off, partially because he felt he was saying too much, and because that ramble of his was expelled in one breath, and he could utter no more.

"I don't think I'd like to be so marked."

"Well, I think you should like to be," he leaned towards her, though she was busy and not looking at him. "It's fascinating, and I think such a feature becomes you. I've never seen freckles on the lips before…"

"… oh… "

And he'd never seen a woman blush so red before. It made him feel weak, and then when she said no more, he began to worry that he'd said something wrong, or that he was just thinking too much now. She showed no signs of real distress, but she was a slippery one when it came to expressing discomfort.

He started to feel sick again, so he excused himself to go out and cool his face, and retrieve the tools he'd forgotten outside.

In bed, he lay awake into the midnight hour, wondering again if he had somehow injured Alma.

Surely he had not offended her. She was just so shy and discreet, and she was not easily insulted, though she was quick to tease. In fact, he imagined her teasing him for this paranoid brooding.

When he finally drifted off to sleep, he saw her standing at the end of the street in the twilight as she had that autumn. She was staring into the horizon, and this time, the ruins she gazed upon were not the scattered remains of abandoned farmhouses, but Ashwood Hall, his home. It was disintegrating and sinking into the earth, fading into the clouds.

They were low and dark, like pillars of smoke, and they seemed to be absorbed by her dress. Her skirt and long hair streamed and billowed, but there was no wind. It was a moonless night, but she was perfectly visible.

He came close and kissed her forehead, and she said, "Your father is waiting for you, Michael. This is not your home."

Michael brought her to him, just as he'd wanted to when he was awake. She was cold. He called her name and pulled her head up, but her lovely face was covered in scrapes, cuts, and bruises, and she was dead. He dropped her, and she sank into the ground.

He did not write that dream down right away, because he'd hoped he would forget it soon.

Dr. Webb was sympathetic to Michael and his ruined hands, and was happy to give him a lighter workload that day.

"Though I'd say you should invest in some gloves as well," said he, pointing at Michael's bare hands as he was layering up to go out again.

"I don't like gloves."

Nature humbled him once again. In an hour, he borrowed a pair of ill-fitting wool gloves from James and sulked back outside.

Both Alma and Dr. Webb would be gone most of the day. His tasks were to sort and file documents in the study, deliver a few letters to post, pick up more tobacco, and burn the paper and kitchen waste out back. He tended to the work that needed to be done in town first, while there was daylight.

He could never quite remember what pipe tobacco Dr. Webb preferred, so he'd written it down on a scrap of paper that was meant to be burned and presented it to the clerk at the pharmacy, whose face lit up when he approached the counter. It was pleasant to know he was missed.

"You work for Dr. Webb, right?" The clerk asked, as she served another handful of customers.

"Yes ma'am, I have for a while. I'm surprised you hadn't noticed."

"Oh, Henry Webb! I remember when he was a minister at the church, almost thirteen years ago," the old man buying his snuff and peppermint drops turned around to look at Michael.

"Yes, 'tis a shame he left," an old lady behind him shook her head. "He was well-loved."

"Why did he leave?" Michael was not often inclined to listen to gossip, but he was curious now.

"Oh, everybody knows—" the man started before he was elbowed by the woman he was with.

"You'd have to ask him yourself, son. Only he can tell you that."

Frankly it made no difference to him, as it was his own business if he decided to leave the church, and the doctor was a good man in his eyes; he had been far kinder to him than he could have asked for.

… was there some past sin he was trying to atone for?

He decided he would ask him about it if he remembered to, and put it out of his mind. That was easy to do, as he had a terrible memory.

He also bought a box of chocolate while he was there, the most expensive he could find, and asked for it to be wrapped in the pretty silver paper they had. It was free this month.

"You know, young man," the clerk leaned her greying head towards his ear as she wrapped his box. "Little Miss Alma Webb helps out over here every Thursday, and she mentions you sometimes."

"She does? What does she say?"

"Nothing much. She does not speak ill of you, if that's what concerns you. She thinks you're a fine gentleman, and a great help."

Heat bloomed in his face. It wasn't tremendous praise, but it tickled him nonetheless.

The clerk bound the papers in ribbons and tied them off in an intricate knot before handing his package to him.

"And who are these for, that you had them done up so nice and pretty?"

"Well, since it was free to wrap them, I just took advantage of the service. And what a lovely job! Thank you very much, that is all," he took the box and departed before she could say something to make him blush even more. The midday breeze cooled his flushed cheeks.

Michael was most certainly not seeking her out, and he definitely was not legitimately plotting revenge, but when he happened to find Ida twirling about on the street that day, he could not pass up the opportunity.

She was wearing a rich purple coat that he had never seen before.

"Did you come back because you just missed me so terribly?" when she saw him, Ida marched right up to him ready to be a nuisance.

"I came back to protect this town from your reign of terror. Did Alma make you that coat?"

"Wouldn't you like to know?"

Well, that was on him for not expecting her to be difficult, but she quickly noticed the parcel under his arm and at once reverted to feigned sweetness.

"Say there, what's in that box?"

"Nothing for you, I'm certain, but I do have something for you as a matter of fact, so come here."

"What?" common sense was not one of her strengths, and she advanced readily.

He brought his fist up and flicked her right between the eyes.

She squealed and rubbed her brow. "That wasn't fair!"

"Of course it's fair, I'd even consider us even now!" he called over his shoulder, as the stun left her distracted so that he could walk away unimpeded. "Had a nice ring to it, by the way! It must be hollow!"

He was chased down the street with a pelting of rocks and a tirade of some not very ladylike squawking. Alma had her work cut out for her, for sure.

And he found her at home earlier than he'd expected. His first clue was a big pot left simmering on the stove, and a mechanical rattling noise brought him to the workroom behind the parlour, Mrs. Webb's old sewing room.

Alma was at the sewing machine, stitching together two panels of pearly linen. A spread of pattern papers and heaps of material were sprawled across the table.

He stood and waited for her to finish an edge and take a break before he spoke:

"So, you *are* getting married, yes?"

"Not necessarily," she smoothed the cloth and adjusted her glasses without looking up. "But I'm preparing a dress in advance. It won't be anything elaborate."

Elaborate would not have suited her tastes, anyway. She sloppily trimmed the excess.

Michael felt that a burden of urgency had been lifted from his shoulders. Why? It wasn't he who faced the prospect of getting married. It made no difference to him.

"That's a lovely fabric."

"It is, isn't it? I bought it with my first wages. I've been saving every little bit I get from working at the pharmacy."

It was so very like her to get paid to hand sweets to children.

"Did you make Ida's new coat?"

"What? No, I've never really sewed all that much until now. Mama helped me get started, and those are the pieces I've been practising on," she gestured to a pile of old cut up fabric that had been stitched until it could be stitched no more.

"I'll leave you to it, and finish up my work."

"Alright, thank you, sir."

"Oh— and you left a pot on the stove, I think."

"I know I did. That's a stew for supper, it needs to cook all afternoon."

He left the chocolate in his room for the time, and took the tobacco upstairs into the study with him. The sewing machine continued.

Dinner was just bread and butter, but that was fine with him. The stew smelled fantastic, and he could not wait to taste it.

Michael ended up saving the fire for last, just to see it at nighttime. He started a little flame, and it lapped up the papers he fed it until it grew into a magnificent, dancing blaze. Even James had come out to appreciate it.

Dr. Webb was home at eight o'clock, and Alma had dutifully set out his fresh supper and a bourbon and water for him when he came in the door. She made a delicious root vegetable stew with thinly sliced vinegared beef that fell apart on the spoon. Michael could not shake the feeling that he was forgetting something. He had only one thing on his mind that afternoon.

After supper, he sat on his bed with the parcel in his lap. He did not know what qualified as good chocolate. He never had it very often, as on the rare occasion that he ate sweets, he was partial to marzipan or little fruit jellies. From what he remembered, it was somewhat bitter, but Alma must have liked bitterness if she could drink plain coffee and enjoy it.

The real challenge was presenting them to her. Every time he resolved to go out and find her, his nerves turned against him and rooted him to his place.

This was ridiculous. It was nearly nine o'clock. The doctor had come and already retired to his study; she was bound to turn in soon, and he'd been in the same spot for nearly two hours.

He sprang up and shut the door behind him in one fluid motion before he had time to stop himself. What was the worst she could say?

Alma was in the sewing room, putting things away, laying out the skeleton of her dress, and shooing Sophie away from it. She turned around and saw him standing in the doorway.

"Ah, Mr. Bennett. I was about to have a cup of coffee before bed. Would you like some?"

"No, you slimy little salamander!" he stood to one side so she could pass with her furry friend in tow. "But if you'd set out some water or milk, I'd gladly accept."

She took her coffee cup into the parlour, and he was just itching to get rid of his box by that point. It grew hot in his hands, and that was not just his anticipation. He'd even left it outside for a minute to make sure it was not too soft.

Alma sat and enjoyed her coffee without a care. It seemed that as long as she had coffee, her Bible, her calico gown, and a cat, then all was right with the world. Since she was not busy or in a visibly prickly mood, this seemed to be the best time to bother her.

Though, what should he say? Nothing? Drop the parcel in her lap and leave like she did in September?

He had to make up his mind soon. She kept looking at him out of the corner of her eye, though she did not seem bothered by him, and was probably accustomed to him staring at her like a madman by now.

"Alma… " he leaned forward and gently touched her wrist. She lifted her head and adjusted her glasses again.

"Ah, um…" he bit his lip and began to feel sick again.

"Sir, say something or don't, please. Is something wrong?"

"Here, this is for you, Alma," Michael handed her the parcel, and as soon as it left his hands, his arms trembled.

She removed the ribbon as neatly as it was fastened and opened each fold of paper individually.

In other words, just slow enough to make him impatient.

"Would you like some help?"

Her lips parted very slightly, and her eyebrows lifted. For her, this was a pretty intense reaction.

"What is this?" She asked.

"What does it look like?"

"I've never had these before!" Alma opened the box, and the smooth chocolate shells of the little bonbons shone in the lamplight like polished stones.

At least they looked nice enough, but how did they taste? He knew she would be grateful for any gift she received, but he would not be satisfied until he saw whether or not he'd made a good choice.

"Well, have them now," he took one out of its chamber and held it up. She took it with her fingers, and did not eat straight from his hand, as he partially hoped she would…

It was worth the money he spent just to see her face light up when she tasted it.

"My, these are wonderful!" she cooed and reached for her mug. "And they're perfect for my coffee!"

Awful creature. How could she ruin his present by adding coffee to it?

"They are?"

"Taste one," she thrust the box right under his nose.

He shook his head. "I bought those for you, not for me."

"And I can do what I want with them."

He took one just to please her. He did not care much for chocolate, but he would still eat it.

He'd had it by itself before, and now he felt foolish for shunning it without trying it this way. The shell burst and gushed a silky raspberry jam that was perfectly sweet and sour.

Alma giggled at whatever strange expression he was making and beckoned him to eat another.

The second one he ate was filled with marzipan, his most favourite thing in the world. That was that. He was a changed man.

The cat took a curious sniff and decided that they were not for it.

Alma seemed much more delighted to share them than to eat them by herself, so she made him have one more. It was marshmallow. That was not quite as good as the others, but not bad. The taste was mild and inoffensive, but he did not like the texture.

After about a third of the box had been finished off, she put the lid back on it and wrapped it back up in its papers.

"Those are fun! But I'll save the rest for later," she set it aside and finished her coffee.

"I'm very pleased that you liked them, then," Michael washed the sweetness from his mouth with a sip of water and silently praised himself just a little. A well-received gift made one's heart feel like a pot about to boil over.

"Well, thank you!"

Michael received the shock of his life when Alma threw her hands upon his neck and planted a kiss right under his chin.

His head was spinning. His hands were sweaty and stiff. Now what did he do? Could he give her one back? Where? How his heart raced!

He lunged forward and kissed that forehead as he'd done in his dream.

She gave a little squeak at the contact. Her face and ears were flaming red, brighter than the fire in the hearth, and she lifted her hands up to cover her mouth. Even her fingers glowed.

He bit down hard on his lip to remain composed (if that's what he was now) and avoid giggling like a lunatic. She was precious. He wanted to kiss every bit of her that he could find, but he was content just to see the rosy bloom of her face.

He watched for just a moment, to take the image with him in his slumber, and decided to take leave before shame could catch up to him. "Well, I will see you tomorrow, Miss Alma," he rose up and quitted the parlour.

His footsteps felt so light and soft, like he was floating away into the clouds until dread pulled him back down to earth as he climbed into bed.

But the image of that one dream came back to him as soon as he put out the candle. He felt her cold, beaten corpse weighing him down, and he could not shake her off. It made him afraid to close his eyes. He heard the ghastly whispers in the stillness of the night…

"Your father is waiting for you, Michael. This is not your home."

X

Thankfully, he had no dreams that night that he could remember, but he did not feel he'd slept at all. At least it was a Sunday, so he was in no rush, and could lie in bed until noon if he wanted.

Why did he feel so dreadful and ill? He was not unhappy with what he did, though he was apprehensive about seeing Alma again. She could be heard bustling about the house at the same time that she always did, but what was she thinking? What did she think about him, especially since he had left so abruptly?

Though he was hungry, he skipped breakfast and sat in his room until Alma and Dr. Webb went off to church. He thought of her in her good green town dress, with her dark blue gloves for a wintry touch, and her cape fastened at her throat. It was probably billowing in the wind like the wings of an angel. He loved her.

James was nowhere to be seen. He rarely was, anyway. Michael's only company was Sophie, coiled up on the couch in the parlour. He sat beside it— her— and stroked her since he had little better to do.

The late Lord Bennett never allowed indoor pets, as much as he adored and sanctified nature; there were just too many valuable relics in the house, and he believed that unless they needed nursing or shelter from the elements, they simply belonged outside. Michael's only exposure to an indoor cat up until now was a peer's mass of white fluff that scratched the back of his neck.

Though he was apprehensive of Sophie, she didn't shed as much as he imagined she would, and soon began purring as he fondled her ears and tail. Maybe she wasn't so bad.

Alma and Dr. Webb came home at half past noon… with Ida. It was not as disastrous as Michael thought it would be, because under her cousin's watch, she was fairly subdued and surprisingly content to quietly practise knitting by the hearth.

"No balls bouncing off of all the furniture today, Miss Ida?" Michael stood over her and watched her poorly attempt to knit a little scarf.

"Toys are for babies. I'm a grown lady."

"Some lady you are, sprawled out on the floor as if you were raised in a barn. Even the cat is up on the couch."

"My mama says animals don't belong on the furniture."

"Maybe you're in the right place, then."

She threw one of her little boots at him. That was the Ida he knew.

"If we were outside, I'd throw it right back at you," Michael sneered and placed the boot on the floor next to its sister. "But I'm a gentleman, and we're in the house."

Well, the fact that she was even sitting still was a miracle of its own. Had Alma used her wondrous menthol panacea to cleanse the demons from her soul?

She disappeared into the sewing room for much of the afternoon, and unlike Ida, he did not want to bother her.

Dr. Webb sat in the parlour and kept Ida occupied for a little while by reading to her, making rings when he blew out smoke, and trying to explain the process of combustion to her (she had asked him what smoke was made of, and immediately stopped listening when he began using words larger than three syllables). She sometimes got up and followed the cat around, or pestered James. He was playing cards by himself, and he had learned to ignore her

entirely, thus he was no fun. She left him soon
enough.

James went into the kitchen with the intention to
prepare dinner. That made Michael a bit nervous
at first, but it turned out that he was only heating
up last night's stew, so it was alright: more than
alright, actually. The doctor was correct in
saying that stew is even better on the second
day.

Most of all, he both dreaded and hoped that he
would speak to Alma again that day. He wanted
to see if she would seek him if he shunned her,
but he couldn't keep it up any longer. She was
successfully coaxed out to have something to
eat, but then Ida consumed almost all of her
attention. It was agony, being within arm's reach
of her, hardly being able to get even one word
in.

Ida was bundled up and kissed all over her awful
face, and given a piece of the chocolate *he* gave
Alma before she was sent home. It made
Michael wonder if his kiss was of the same
nature. Was he another little pet to her?

There was only one way to find out. And as
usual, he figured it would be best for him to
approach her while she was alone.

Feeding the chickens out in the barn was not ideal, but he was too impatient. He put on his coat in case he would be out for a while, then crept up to the little side door and waited for her. It would probably be well to invite her on a walk at that time, as he knew she loved the sunset just as much as he did.

She almost dropped her bucket when she emerged and saw him standing there. Maybe he should not have stood in the shadows and scared her half to death.

"Sorry, I didn't mean to startle you," he stepped into the light. "Are you perhaps bundled up suitably, and willing to take a little walk?"

Alma looked at him, at the house, out into the street, and back at him. Her lips parted and then sealed again. Did she not trust him?

"I won't take you very far."

"Alright," she put the bucket down, clasped her hands at her waist, and waited, as she would not lead; she never did.

"Come with me, then," he urged softly and offered his left arm.

To his surprise, she hooked her little hands onto his arm (all of her touches were a surprise to him) and followed two or three steps behind.

"I wish you would walk at my side, instead of right behind me. Am I too fast for you?"

"I feel secure back here, sir."

"Well, I don't feel secure if I can't see my travelling companions, especially when they are so little."

She came closer— much closer. She twined both her arms onto his elbow and pressed into his side.

"Are you cold?" he turned to look at her now that he could actually see her.

"No."

He stopped at the street and looked out in both directions. Should they walk into town or out the other way, into the hills and ruins?

He walked towards the hills, but she resisted and dug her feet into the ground.

"I want to go the other way."

"Why? It's towards the old houses you like to look at, and it will be less crowded."

"No, I don't want to go that way!" she tugged him back.

Alma started into the darkness as if she gazed upon death itself. She was not merely being stubborn; she sounded so fearful that it froze him where he stood.

"What did you see that makes you not want to go over there?"

"I… I saw… somebody was watching me," she murmured in such a hauntingly low and chilling tone, and she trembled like a leaf in the wind. "I saw somebody watching me out there."

Michael only knew of one watchful pair of eyes in that town, and the body they resided in could have been snapped as easily as straw in his thumb and forefinger.

Was that all? By her tone, he'd think she just witnessed a murder. Still, he left unarmed, and he wanted her to be perfectly at ease.

"You scare easily, don't you?" he turned the other direction, towards the dim streetlights. "Well, you are safe with me."

Admittedly, he was on edge. He never felt completely secure walking around at night anyway, but she was so mortally frightened by whatever watched her some time ago, and it made him think of… that dream.

There must have been more she was not telling him, but he would not press.

She seemed alright now that they were headed into town. Her spirits were immediately lifted, and she gazed out at the vibrant, bloody red December sunset. The official end of autumn was the solstice, but the spirit of winter was upon them already.

"And you don't mind being seen with me at this hour?" he asked and pointed towards the buildings. "It seems these folks delight in gossip."

"You are a well-respected gentleman, sir, and they know you work for my father."

He used to think his status compelled him to be held to a higher standard of conduct, but as the weight of his rank seemed to grow lighter by the day, he was more inclined to hold himself to a set of standards not because he was supposed to, but because he wanted to. So he was a gentleman? A gentleman is made by his manner, not his station— at least that is what his father told him.

"And what are you? What do they think of you?"

"I'm the doctor's daughter, sir. Nothing more, nothing less. Ida has more of a reputation than me, especially among the elderly. She bats her little eyes and the old folks give her a half penny for sweets."

"Probably paying her to go away."

"You must admit she is much improved as of late."

"I suppose so, and I also suppose that was no small feat on your part."

"I temper her a bit."

She was far too modest. It was almost irritating.

"Give yourself more credit. You practically raise her, among the rest of your obligations."

"It's no obligation, sir. I look after her because I want to."

"Of course you do, you are a little darling, aren't you?"

She now gazed right up at him with her large, inquisitive eyes.

He watched her from the corner of his.

"If you look at me like that, I might kiss you again."

She stared harder, if that was possible, in a most audacious manner, with raised brows, as if challenging him.

They weren't in the middle of town yet, and the house was quite far off as well.

Michael kissed her forehead; that was a safe place. She giggled. He kissed her scalp, her cheek, and her nose, and she gasped and squealed with her hands over her mouth, and leaned into his side. She hid her face in his coat, but he could still reach behind her ear.

He may have stood out in the dark and kept kissing her, but he felt an icy cold needle prick sensation on his nose, and slowly the little tap of freezing rain swelled all around them. So much for their walk.

"Damn, and on the one day I didn't wear a hat!" He seized one of Alma's hands and turned on his heels, running towards the house as fast as he could manage with her in tow.

The street was slick and shining when they made it to the stile, and it was a pitiful slog to trudge up the wet hill to the house. He was not thoroughly soaked, but his neck and face were dripping, and his raw hands burned from the cold.

After he shut and latched the door, he took off Alma's wet cape and rushed her straight to the parlour, where there was a good fire waiting.

Michael grabbed ahold of her hands as she tried to wipe his face off, and held them close to the fire.

"You should worry about warming your hands, Alma. I can handle myself."

As he said this, though, he huddled close against her for her warmth, and took a blanket that had been draped over the couch to cover them with. She was so very close. He could feel her breath.

Alma had been flushed and sheepish only a moment ago, and now she was pale, grave, and reserved, shrinking away from him.

"Are you sick?" he tried to pull more of the blanket onto her. She brushed it off.

"Do you like me, sir?"

"Of course I like you, what a silly question! We are friends, and if it's quite alright, I should like to seek a little more than that."

"Young men of your station, I'm told, are accustomed to seeking thrills and passing fancies. What am I?"

That stung him. He felt misjudged and misunderstood. Of all the vices that plagued men of leisure— lavishness, pride, greed, debauchery— he abhorred debauchery.

"Philandery is completely beneath me. The day you catch me engaging in such coquetry, which I dare say shall never be realised— load up a rifle and put me out of my misery."

She blinked her eyes hard.

"You can use mine. I'll show you how."

"I don't think I'd be able to lift it, sir."

"You needn't call me that all the time. Give me my Christian name. Call me Michael."

"This doesn't feel real."

"It is real, indeed," he brought her close enough for her to feel his feverish and ardent heartbeat. "Do you not believe me?"

"If your offer is genuine, I accept it, Michael."

His name on her breath was sweeter than the lightest notes of any harp or flute. He would give anything to hear it continuously.

If he kissed those quivering lips right now, they would be his first, and that would seal his words.

Michael brought his face down so that their noses touched, and he hesitated to see if she would withdraw. Alma shuddered, and he thought she would pull away from him, but she didn't. He kissed her, and it was softer than any sensation he'd felt before, but still so very cold. Would he thaw the frozen woman, or would she freeze him?

He kissed her a second time, and he ruined it by mashing her lips and grinding their teeth together, but it made her laugh.

They were not alone. She alerted him that they were being watched, not with her words, but with her eyes. He followed her apprehensive gaze and found the shadowy form of the old doctor leaning against the doorway, with an amazed and confused expression that Michael had never seen before.

"Hello, Papa," Alma fluttered her little fingers.

He nodded and vanished as silently as he had entered the parlour.

Michael possibly had some explaining to do…

"Perhaps I should go to bed," Alma stood up and smoothed her dress.

He didn't want her to go to bed. He wanted to sit there with her until morning. This night was perfect, and he wanted it to last forever.

But he knew they both had to work tomorrow.

"Wait— before you go," he riveted her to him and kissed all over her forehead. "Goodnight," he kissed both her cheeks, around her eyes. "Goodnight, Alma."

"Goodnight," she gathered up her shawl and slipped away, leaving the door ajar.

It was hard for him to fall asleep, not from terror or brooding, but giddiness like no other. He went to bed with no fear and no regrets, neither was he plagued by the burden of obligations and an uncertain future. What did this new chapter

mean for his aspirations? He would worry about
it later. His dreams were of sweet springtime,
and her loose hair in the wind.

XI

Breakfast was not as light and easy as his dreams. There was a heavy, foreboding air over the silence at the table. Alma's discomfort was tangible as she tried to fill that air with little comments about last night's rain, questions about how everybody slept, and offers to refill somebody's cup. He humoured her as best as he could, but she eventually just gave up and finished her meal quietly.

The potatoes were not thoroughly and evenly cooked, and the eggs were not salted. She was clearly distracted. Nobody complained.

Dr. Webb presented Michael with his work for the day as she cleared the table. He had mail to deposit and a barn to finish, as the task had been largely neglected since last Friday. When he studied the doctor's mein, he did not seem angry (at least not at Alma) more than he was agitated and nervous.

She tried to retreat back into her room as soon as the dishes were washed, but her father called her upstairs. Michael was fastening his coat by the staircase and smiled at her as she passed. He got a little smile in return, but he did not draw a vibrant blush out of her as he'd hoped.

He, too, was distracted while he worked. Of course he was worried that the doctor may upset Alma, but he was also concerned that if he was driven from the house, he would lose his security and be set back in his plans. Even sleeping in the outhouse in the dead of winter would be preferable to being cast off. Abraham would have taken him in without a second thought, but that was out of the question. He could not make himself a burden to the old man, and he also did not want an earful each day about his "skewed priorities."

Well, if he would have to toil for seven or fourteen years like Jacob, so be it. After he had just confirmed his devotion to her, he could not leave her.

He took a break from the work on the barn to post a letter. This one was addressed to Abraham. What would Abraham and the doctor have to talk about? Did it have anything to do with him or his father? It took a tremendous amount of willpower not to open it.

The dreaded Albert Gillman was by the inn that day, with his hands in his pockets. He was looking every which way with no rhyme or reason in his gaze until he saw Michael, and shrank away. Was he really that intimidating?

Maybe Michael should attempt to strike up a conversation. He knew nothing about him, after all.

"Good day, sir," he tipped his hat. "Going somewhere?"

"N-no," Gillman stammered in a soft and mild voice, like a child that had been caught stealing a piece of pie.

"Fine weather today. Not too wet."

"No— yes."

Gillman's usual slack and relaxed expression changed from fear to annoyance very quickly. This was clearly going nowhere.

"Well, take care, then."

"Yes."

A very stimulating discussion. Not that he expected much more, but it removed some of that sense of mystery. Albert Gillman was just a strange man with a pretty face, and undoubtedly many local connections. It wasn't hard to imagine he'd have a slew of women pawing at him, had he possessed a charming wit to match the well-made vessel.

Well, Michael only knew of one creature that was blessed in such a way.

While he was out, he took the liberty of buying more tea for the house. He wanted something hot to drink, and he wanted to never touch coffee again if he could help it.

Since he had hot beverages on his mind, he went back to the inn, into the tavern with a craving for their cider. Gillman was not there. He went inside and ordered it spiced and hot. It was much nicer in winter than it was in summer, almost a suitable substitute for his prized mulled wine. The innkeeper was pleased to see him drink with more enthusiasm.

Of course, he had to swallow it quickly and then go home to finish the barn before it got too dark. He'd have to come back and order it again when he wasn't busy, but it thoroughly warmed his bones for the walk back.

Michael finished the rest of his work faster than he thought he would, and his hands weren't terribly sore. He was not home for dinner, so he was quite famished by the time he put the tools away.

What had Alma been up to all day?

He looked for her, but she was not in the kitchen, the sewing room, or the parlour, and neither was her cat. She must have been in her room, and he would not dare try to go in there.

"Michael, there you are!" Dr. Webb descended from the second storey and stopped at the bottom of the staircase. He wasn't wearing his wool smoking jacket. Truly a rare sight. "You're late. Has something happened?"

"No, sir, I just bought a little tea while I was out," he held up the box.

"Well, that's very considerate of you. Ah, put it in the kitchen, and then come upstairs. I need to speak with you."

The doctor went back up the stairs without waiting for him. The door to the study was open, so that's where he went. Dr. Webb shut the door behind him.

He sat down and produced his box of cigars. "Will you take one?"

Just the sight of them made him want to retch, and troubled his already nervous stomach.

"No thank you, sir."

"Right, right," he put the cigars back and laced his fingers together on the desk. "Sit down, then."

That was not a polite invitation. It was the tone of a father about to reprimand his son. Michael felt he simply could not resist, and obeyed him. His legs would not fit normally under the desk, but if he moved the chair further away, he might have appeared hostile, so he just conceded to the discomfort. It was nothing compared to how he chafed inwardly in that moment.

He would not speak unless he was spoken to. An eternity of silence fit into maybe eight seconds.

"So you seem to be involved with Alma in some way."

"Yes, sir."

That was all he dared to say.

"She is very fond of you, and had only kind things to say about you. She is quite young, though, and not acquainted with young men, and has been warned to be on her guard about you."

That seemed unfair. Michael thought he had proven himself to be a reliable and honest fellow.

But he also knew that every father felt an obligation to issue such a warning to their daughters, so he tried not to be offended. That being the case, he was not sure how to respond, either…

So he did not.

"And as for you," Dr. Webb spread his hands upon the table, with his palms up. "I like you Michael, so I will only say this much: I advise you to be sure of yourself. She is yet too young to marry, but I think she will someday. If you do not think you would ever be prepared to marry her, do not waste her time."

Now that was certainly unfair. He had a genuine love for her, and he was being spoken of as if he were some skirt-chaser.

"Sir, Alma is everything that suits me and pleases me. I can't imagine the likeness of a woman I would be more inclined to marry, and I doubt my feelings will change."

"Well, that is a comfort if it is not an empty promise, but there is one more thing I wanted to discuss, in that regard."

"Sir?"

"You have lived on my property for nearly six months, and have been in my house for about three. I pay you quite handsomely for your workload, and I don't charge you for your room and board. Don't misunderstand me, I do enjoy your company, and I know it takes time for you young people to get on your own feet; but you have not shown any signs of moving up in the world, and you seem to have no goals, no purpose. Even if you wanted to marry her right this minute, I would turn you away on that basis alone."

That was brutal. And it made sense. It just occurred to him that he had not told a soul about his funds or his plans for them, other than Abraham. He would perhaps be a bit more understanding and even sympathetic if he told him.

"Well, sir, I am immensely grateful for the help you have given me— more than I can say, really. I am indebted to you and your household. For that reason, I trust you enough to confide in you. What I've not told you, all this time, is that as of now I have about seven thousand in the bank that I've scarcely touched."

Henry Webb's upturned hands flipped over to slap down hard on the desk.

"Seven thousand pounds, Michael?" he rubbed his eyes from the shock, and then adjusted his glasses, as if those were numbers he could see. "That is a high aristocrat's annual salary. You could be set up well enough to take up a decent trade and acquire your own house. You could travel the world if you pleased. Why are you even here?"

"My land was seized by the government months ago, and I had to sell my family's house that has been ours for centuries," passion rose within him as he spoke. "It is a blight on my name to be driven from my own home. But I have more than half of the funds required to buy back just the manor. In time, I should soon be able to buy back Ashwood Hall!"

Dr. Webb furrowed his brow. The corners of his moustache twitched, as if he was about to laugh.

"So you'll slave away for twenty or thirty years, buy back Ashwood… and then what?"

"Then what? That is it, sir. I will have fulfilled my obligations to my family name and paid the debt I owe to myself."

"Michael, I don't believe you've thought this through," he leaned forward and held his hands out again. "I knew you must not be wise to the ways of the world, but my God, man… you don't have a real living. You probably don't know how to handle your finances. What will you do? Do you plan to buy it back, only to die alone and penniless in a big, empty house?"

Michael felt very small, and completely helpless. Abraham's fears and warnings were coming back to him. More than that, it dawned on him just how much he had to learn about the world. Taxes and such had not even crossed his mind.

It was either the spirit of perseverance or blind stubbornness, but he was not defeated. He was unskilled and uneducated at the time, yes, but he could better himself… still, he needed help.

"Sir," he was about to beg, but he remained composed and did not grovel. "I know my workload is light for my wages… but if I show you that I am committed to learning and improving myself, could I please continue living here as I do now?"

The doctor narrowed his eyes, gazing out the window. He sighed and rose from his chair. Michael stood as well, only because he felt it was proper.

"If you were not the son of a dearly departed friend, I would have begun charging you rent a long time ago. You should thank Alma for putting a portion of her wages towards our food, meagre as they are. And speaking of Alma— you say you would marry her, yes?"

"Yes, sir."

"That is all well. But you will not— you cannot marry her until you have set up residence elsewhere and are no longer dependent on me. Do we understand each other, Michael?"

"We understand each other, sir."

"Good," Dr. Webb reached out his hand, and Michael took it. "Now then, let us go down and have some of that tea."

"Yes, sir," he'd probably said *sir* more times in those few minutes than he had on any single day in his life, but while he knew his burden was about to drastically increase, he felt a great sense of relief as well.

Father, I will be home soon, he sent his thoughts into the earth.

Dr. Webb dismissed him, and then Michael hobbled away to walk off the numbness in his legs.

Michael had hoped Alma would linger in the parlour late at night as she often did, and he found her, indeed.

She was on the couch, reading her bible by the firelight, in that old dress he was starting to love. Surprisingly, there was no cat.

He moved her hair to one side and pressed his cheek to her velvety soft neck. Over her shoulder, he saw she was reading Luke.

"Will you read to me again?"

"Will you listen?"

"I cannot guarantee anything. It can't be helped if your angelic voice lulls me to sleep."

"Very well," Alma began to read aloud in the most flat and grating voice that she could manage. She could not finish half of a page before he began to laugh.

She shut the book. "That was a fruitless endeavour," she put it on the side table and reclined onto his outstretched arm.

"I wanted to see you all day," he cooed and pulled her closer.

"What did my father say to you?"

"He said that I cannot marry you until I am completely independent and have taken up a decent trade. I accept these conditions."

"That is all fine and well. I feel I shall not be married for a while, anyway."

"You are not aching to be my bride?"

"Sir, you are not suitable for marriage as of now. Nor am I."

"You want me to be a fervent missionary husband? Will you convert me, one bible reading at a time?"

She shook her head. "I only want you to be yourself, sir, but I think we can all strive to be the best version of ourselves."

"A fair answer, but were you not telling me months ago that you ached to spread the word of God to the uncontacted peoples of Africa?"

She pinched up her brow and adjusted herself to lean more comfortably on his arm.

"I see a necessity in spreading the word of God, which would be most efficiently done if I remain a spinster, but if I am meant to marry and stay in England, I will abide. The duty of a Christian wife is sacred, and just as much of a calling as any other."

"That, it may be. If I had you as a wife, you would be sacred indeed. I would treasure you like no other woman, above all things—"

"Sir," she interrupted. "Do not place the instrument higher than He who ordains it. Do not seek me in the stead of God."

"You liar! You said you did not want to change me, and you steer me straight to church."

"And neither do I, because I know that I cannot. I want you to seek your Maker who cares for you. He can plant the seeds of change within you if He sees fit. I cannot force you to choose Him, I would only prefer it."

She was a woman who sought the Lord. Well, he was a Lord: the Lord of seven thousand pounds, soon to be the Lord of Ashwood Hall once again.

The alternative was the Lord of all Creation. Perhaps the odds were not stacked in his favour.

There was a part of him clamouring to be anything she wanted him to be, but a respectable facade constructed to please her would be dishonest and easily torn down. He should have just been grateful that a gentle dream of a creature was content to nestle into his arms that evening.

Currently, he wanted nothing to change, as sitting by the fire with his sweet Alma was all he desired, even if she delighted in confusing him. Maybe Michael was afraid of change, and everything he had worked for being taken from him.

The one thing he *was* willing to change at that moment was the topic of conversation.

"When neither of us is busy," he began and smoothed her hair away from her face. "Suppose I take you into town, or maybe even to London. You could have some ladies make a wedding dress for you."

"Well, I want to make my own dress."

"But you could have a train longer than the aisle of a cathedral, in shimmering pearly satin or snowy white gossamer— anything you want—"

"I don't want any of that, I want to make my own dress. It must be made with what I bought myself, and by my own hands."

"What might I buy you, then?"

"Nothing. I have everything that I need. I would gladly go into town with you while you purchased to your heart's content, but I ask for nothing, and expect nothing."

"Spoiling you will be more difficult than I thought it would be."

And why should he spoil her? His funds were meant for his future, not some farm girl… this beautiful farm girl…

He wanted her to be his future as well…

If Alma wasn't a part of his future, then he would be perfectly content if the sun never rose tomorrow. If she was his past, he would always be pining for yesterday. All he had was today.

So be my present, at the very least.

There was a sort of haughty stubbornness in her taut lip, as if it amused her to refuse him. It drew him out of his brooding moodiness.

The fire was low, but she was plenty warm. She pressed her face into his shirt. Her hair smelled of cinnamon. He lifted her head up for a kiss— at least one.

Well, he couldn't stop at just one. He seized her by her arms and figured he'd managed to kiss

just about every bit of her face before she had
bent all the way back in her squirming and was
completely flushed and breathless from tittering
and squealing.

"Let me up. I want some water," Alma prodded
at him, and he realised he had her arm pinned
down under his elbow.

Michael became aware of his surroundings again
when he sobered up, and only just now thought
of all the noise they'd made. He hoped they
hadn't disturbed anyone.

He did not actually want to stop, but he learned
something new, at least. The fact that she could
be wrought to such a fit just by kissing her face
was… intriguing.

When she came back, the colour was still on her
cheeks.

"Goodnight, sir. I'll be going to bed now," she
extinguished the lamp. The only light left was
from the moon and the last flickering tongue of
fire in the hearth.

"Goodnight, Alma," he caught her in the hall and
stole one more little kiss from her.

She turned to go to her chamber, but he stood in
his place and held onto her hand.

"It's very cold. Do you want to sleep in my bed?"

She started and pulled her fingers free.

"I do not!"

He cringed, fearing he said something wrong, and then he felt affronted.

"What sort of rake do you take me for? I don't beat around the bush! I speak my intentions clearly. If I wanted any more than that, I'd have asked for it."

"Oh? If I misjudged you, I'm sorry."

He cleared his throat.

"Now, once more; would you like to *sleep* in my bed?"

"Once more, no."

"You don't trust me?"

"I like my bed to myself."

"Very well. That is your business."

"Good night."

"Good night."

She disappeared into her room, her forbidden chamber. Michael wanted to follow her. He wanted to lie down beside her and fall asleep to the sound of her breath; that was all.

And that was the way it went for many weeks. They exchanged a few words at the kitchen table, they worked in the daytime, and they came together for an hour or two at night. They talked, he advanced, and she met him first with caution, then with enthusiasm. He was sent to bed half delirious with her kisses, half poisoned by the sting of her blunt remarks, and wholly wishing there was just one more hour in the day.

XII

Unbeknownst to Michael at that time, he was scarcely concerned with his estate, or any such affairs. He didn't have the time to dwell on it. Dr. Webb had instructed him to choose a practical skill that seemed appealing to him, and carpentry was most attractive. He took up an apprenticeship in town when he was not working for the doctor, and he came home exhausted, plucking splinters out of his hands. Despite that, he always set aside some minutes for Alma.

Never had he sought after somebody so fervently. He even found himself attending church on her behalf. Strange as it seemed, there was a contagious and charming energy upon her as he watched her in her prayers. He marvelled at it, and sometimes even envied it. As for her, she seemed delighted to have that quiet sway over him.

As the nights grew colder, he appreciated her warmth more and more, but he wished that most of their time was not confined to late night meetings in the parlour. It made him feel as if their courtship was illicit and scandalous, especially since she would not accept caresses in the presence of others. His father never had any trouble drawing sweetness from his mother.

With Michael, however, affection was not so natural between them…

But Christmas was drawing nearer. He had five days to produce a suitable gift for Alma. Abraham and the Webb gentlemen were easy. He did not feel pressured to impress them. Men of their ilk liked simple things.

Alma, on the other hand, did not seem to be concerned about presents at all, and never had a definitive answer when asked what she wanted. It was irksome indeed. All he wanted was to indulge her.

She once asked him to bring her undyed wool fabric, which he did gladly. What would she make with it? Was it a rustic addition to her wedding dress? He often dreamed of seeing it finished.

He then watched her cut it up and use it to line the inside of a box layered with straw and rags. The box went into a crevice beneath the stairs, where light did not reach.

"Sophie has been looking for a place to nest before she has her kittens," Alma explained. "It won't be long before she gives birth, and she will not want to be disturbed."

Sophie never used the box. She pulled the lining out and kneaded up a lumpy mass on the floor right next to it.

"Alma, I want to give something to *you*, not the cat!" he stopped her in the hall as she was about to cook supper. "What do you want? Something for your bridal ensemble, perhaps? You like jewellery, yes? You wear the same brooch almost every day, so I suppose you don't have much."

"I have other pieces, but I like this brooch," she ran her fingers over the peachy shell cameo head pinned at her throat, down to the third button on her bodice. The gesture tortured him. "You could buy me another if you'd like, though."

That was progress!

"And what do you like? I think gold and silver would both suit you equally; you have such a lovely complexion."

"Brass is economic, and modestly charming."

"Brass will not do. Only the best I can get."

"Buy whatever you'd like, within reason."

"It doesn't matter what *I'd* like! I won't be wearing it!"

"You will be looking at it, won't you?" she approached and nudged her face into his collar. He was now mentally subdued and could not argue. "Buy what you think will look best on me."

That was difficult to determine, because he thought anything would be made beautiful on her. She must have known it as well, and maybe for that reason, she was merely indecisive.

"What would you like me to give you?" she stood away from him now.

"Your love," he gushed and brought her closer by her waist.

"You have that already, sir."

"Tell me straightforward, then. You dance around the subject so often."

"I can do that now. I love you."

"Then I have all that I want. Don't worry about it."

"I will indeed worry about it, but I suppose I will have to surprise you."

"I would cherish anything you have to give, Alma."

"Suppose I bring you a dead patch of thorns from the woods."

"You already give me thorns in the shape of your piquant remarks. Still, I would cradle it to my cheek and weep bloody tears of joy."

She laughed in her usual perplexing way, and pried herself from his grasp. "I really must prepare supper, though."

He left her to her task, but now he had to ponder what jewellery would truly look best on her. That was difficult when she wore so little of it.

But he had an idea of her tastes, and he had a plan.

Money was not all that he had stored away at the bank. Though he'd resorted to selling many precious artefacts from his home, he kept the heirloom jewellery of the ladies of Ashwood.

This was quite advantageous. Firstly, he would not be spending any extra money, which would appease her sensibilities. Secondly, antiquated ornaments would complement her timeless and subdued beauty. Thirdly, and most importantly, he could not think of a more apparent declaration of his love than to lavish her with the gems his mother, grandmother, et cetera.

The reason he had not sold it is because most of it was in the bank, not at home, and it did not occur to him when he first sold the estate. Besides, the collection was such an ancient and intimate relic, that it would have just been something else for him to work assiduously to buy back. He was glad that he didn't sell it.

Now with new resolve, Michael wrote his banker and asked for the jewellery to be delivered to Liverpool. He would retrieve them during his brief visit with Abraham on Christmas eve.

The transaction reminded him that this was his first Christmas without his father. It was perhaps the first time since summer that he came close to weeping. He wiped his tears and sealed the letter. He would deliver it tomorrow.

He began to practise the piano once in a while as well. His mother loved piano and watercolour, and he'd only managed not to ruin one of those. It was hard to visualise given how large and rough they were, but his hands were quite nimble when he didn't have to hold a brush.

Alma sometimes sat on a footstool at his knee and listened to him play. She was a good listener, because she was not proficient enough to point out his mistakes. Her father, on the other hand, was an experienced organist with a fine and stringent ear, and a passion for correcting.

Michael considered that a little music would put the house in a festive mood for the official arrival of winter, and hoped to play well enough to brighten the house for Christmas. There was no tree and few decorations, as that was against Dr. Webb's strictly minimalist and practical tastes. Trees were a hassle to put up, only to be left with a mess later. Ribbons and streamers were clutter. Fruit and grain garlands were wasteful. The best Alma could do was set an ornate arrangement of wax-covered pine cones and evergreen sprigs over the mantelpiece. At least they were fragrant.

The Webb children were gone to visit their mother in those last three days, so Michael would not see Alma until late on Christmas day. He could only hope his banker came through in time.

He and the doctor had the house to themselves the day before he would leave for Liverpool.

That is, except for Sophie and her new kittens. Michael heard their squeaking at many hours of the day, and he still thought they looked like rats. They were instructed by Alma to leave plenty of food at the bottom of the staircase and stay away from the nest to avoid disturbing the cats.

Being alone with Dr. Webb was preferable to being alone with James, because the former was at least a passable cook. It was a bit uncomfortable when Alma was brought up, but the doctor seemed to approve of Michael now.

It surprised him to find that a supposedly fervent Christian man had such little investment in Christmas. Perhaps leaving the ministry was just due to a total or partial loss of faith, which was bound to spark contempt among a mob of elderly busybodies that had lived their whole lives knowing only the church and the plough. Aside from his exacting and overly sceptical nature (which was often checked by his generosity anyway), there seemed to be no faults within him that would warrant unrest in the community. Michael would have to ask for himself, but he could never bring himself to do so.

Abraham's home was much more festive. He did not have the space for a stately Christmas tree, but the parlour was decorated in red, gold, and green. They enjoyed rum and oranges by the fire, and Abraham was pleased that Michael was bettering himself with practical skills. He promised Abraham a place at the estate once he bought it back: not as a servant, but as a treasured friend. He mumbled a passive, "how nice," at Michael's offer.

His gift to Abraham was a few of the fine knives he'd taken from the late Lord Bennett's collection, wrapped in silk. It was of little use to the old man, but it brought forth a rain of sentimental tears, and it took a bit of persuasion to get him to accept it. Michael's eyes welled up, too, as he felt he was giving up a piece of his father, but his friend's glowing face made it worth parting with. His father did not belong to him alone, after all.

Abraham's gift to him was a photograph of a very young Michael, an infant girl, and Lady Bennett, their mother. He had never seen it before; Abraham had kept it all this time.

"That is your sister!" he told Michael. "You, ah— you don't remember?"

He did not remember his sister at all, and it pained him more than he could express as he gazed at her little face and had no impression of her in his mind. His parents never spoke of her. Had he not found this picture, it'd have been as though she didn't exist. Michael looked to be about five years old. He should have remembered her well. Why didn't he?

"Abraham, what was her name?" Michael traced a finger over her outline. "My father never talked about her, I don't remember anything—"

He stopped because his trembling voice warned him to speak no more.

"Ah, her name was Berthe…" Abraham tapped his chin and raised his eyes to the ceiling as he tried to recall. He shuddered, as if realising he had revealed a horrible secret. "Just like your grandmother! Lord Bennett believed she would look just like her. She was a lovely woman in her youth, tall and stately, with shining jetty hair and eyes just as dark. Her father was Italian, you know: Big Black Berthe, they called her; it suited her, as she was always so imposing and dour—"

"That is all well, but Baby Berthe, Abraham," he tapped the photograph. "What was she like?"

"Oh… she was a fat, hardy baby just like you were, at least for a little while. When she was perhaps two months old, she started having awful convulsions, and we could not find out why. After a terrible bout, her little body just went stiff one day, and that was how she died. How helpless your mother and father felt… she suffered her whole life."

Michael could understand why his parents
would not want to speak of such an awful
ordeal, but to conceal it from him felt like
betrayal. It seemed cruel to leave so little of her
in the world. He'd never found a single remnant
of her existence in the house.

"And after that," Abraham continued. "they were
too cautious and hesitant to have any more
children. That is why your father kept you as he
did, even at your detriment. You were his crown
jewel, his pride, and he prolonged even sending
you to college if it meant turning you over to the
world. He even abandoned his dream of steering
you into the military to follow in his footsteps
and his father's, and was content to put you into
boxing instead. You did get into many fights as a
boy, and he at least made that into something
practical."

"So he did," Michael touched the bridge of his
nose, which was crooked from being broken
many times. He hadn't looked straight ahead for
portraits since he was fifteen. It was his only
genuine insecurity, but he'd begun to forget it in
his new environment.

"Michael, do not be angry with your father,"
Abraham entreated him. "He may have made
questionable decisions, but he thought he was
doing the best he could for you, and his
judgement was clouded by his grief and fear."

"I'm not angry, Abraham."

But he was angry. He could not stop himself
from being angry, though he tried to swallow it
down with rum until his skull hummed like a
nest of bees, and he could not hold himself erect.

He excused himself to settle into bed. Again, he
had nobody to trouble with his disturbed
thoughts, so he wrote them down. Scattered
nonsense poured from his heart as an illegible
scratch while he threw down one glass of
alcohol after another. Before he knew it, he'd
finished another bottle.

When he awoke the next morning, he did not
remember what he wrote, nor could he read it.
His pounding-drum headache and sore jaw did
not help.

"Ah, Abraham, my man," he mumbled as he
trudged into the hall and found the old man. "I
drank all of your bottle of rum. I am sorry…" he
inspected the pen he'd used, and found it covered
with strange grooves. "Oh… and it appears I
chewed on one of your pens."

He vomited the alcohol from his system, washed
the bitter taste out of his mouth, and set out at
noon to pick up the jewels he expected, with the
broadest hat he had, and without his hair combed

away from his eyes, squinting like some pale
cave creature. The treasure he sought had
arrived punctually, so brilliant still that they
singed his eyes.

There was a light dusting of powdery snow on
the ground by the time he returned to the Webbs.
Alma was out tending to the chickens, so he had
time to make the present somewhat presentable.

He opened the box and examined each exquisite
piece. There was an assortment of rings,
bracelets, collars, and earrings, crafted in every
manner of shining metal, in delicate thread-like
chains, or sturdy bands and plating. Glittering
gems cut in every shape under the sun were set
perfectly.

Alma would have outshone the Queen in any
one of these sets, but he could not give them all
to her at once; then he would not be able to
surprise her with more. He was sure that not all
of them would suit her tastes anyway, thus he
began the process of sorting and sifting.

This large string of diamonds? She would
probably hate it, and it was so heavy. He was
also sure she did not have pierced ears, so
earrings were off the table. A braided silver
circlet would nest beautifully in her hair, but she
was unlikely to wear it if there was no occasion
for it.

There it was: a small ring of blushing Russian gold, set with a centre piece of milky opal surrounded by freshwater seed pearls the same creamy pink as her skin. A few blemishes were present in the form of tiny scratches, and a distorted, slightly asymmetrical centre. She would probably appreciate these features regardless. It was old, exotic, and softly yet powerfully feminine. It was perfect.

Now that he'd found what he was looking for, the rest of the stash was stored away in a locked casket, along with the picture of his mother and sister.

He kept a sheet of the silvery paper he'd had her chocolates wrapped in. The ring was nestled into a linen handkerchief and then folded into the paper. He hoped she would love it.

The kitchen door opened and slammed shut. She had come in just in time. Michael readied all of the gifts he had to give and left his room.

"You were out in the cold, in your nice new dress?" he heard Dr. Webb call out incredulously from the parlour.

"I had my mantle on, and I didn't get it dirty!" Alma called back.

Nice new dress? This, he most definitely needed to see.

The Webbs were seated in the parlour, with dessert and coffee. A magnificent fire illuminated the room.

Michael stopped in his tracks with one foot in the threshold.

Alma was as dazzling as the fire. No other words could describe her at that moment. She wore a deep crimson dress that hugged her form and flared out below the hips in a tucked drape. Pale blonde lace capped the elbow-length sleeves and low bodice. There were probably more precise terms that a real seamstress could have told them, but he knew none of them. Instead of her usual brooch, she wore a plain band of black velvet at her throat, with matching gloves and her hair in a high coiffure.

He was thankful that he'd changed into his best suit and hand-painted waistcoat before he'd left his room. He'd hate to be so underdressed in her presence.

"Michael, come in and sit down, boy!" Dr. Webb beckoned him over with a wave of his pipe. "You missed dinner, so come and have some of this pudding."

"Ah, merry Christmas, everybody," Michael sat on the couch next to Alma as he was served a generous portion of sweet pudding and a mug of something hot. It wasn't coffee; it was a young red wine with nutmeg and allspice. The taste was modestly pleasing and aromatic, and went well with the pudding. Since the room smelled strongly of coffee, he guessed he was the only person having wine.

His gift to Dr. Webb was a shelf for his study that he made himself over the span of a week. The doctor called it "rugged;" in other words, it was ugly. He still thanked him for it.

For James, he had purchased a small collection of hats. He did not seem to own any, as he never wore them out in the field, and his neck and nose were perpetually scalded bright red. James seemed perplexed at first, but accepted the gift nonetheless. Dr. Webb's hats were used as a size reference when placing his order, it seemed to have yielded serviceable results.

Of course, he was most excited to give Alma her gift. He waited impatiently as she unfolded the paper. It wasn't as if he'd put a great deal of effort into the wrapping, so he didn't know why she bothered taking her time.

She produced the ring at last, and first she turned pure white, then red as the dress she was wearing. Even the doctor whistled appreciatively.

"My word!" he exclaimed and raised his glasses to peer at it. "Michael, where did you get that? Looks foreign to me."

"It's been in my family for at least forty years," Michael replied and gestured for Alma to try it on. "Though I don't know where it came from. I believe my mother purchased it while visiting the continent."

He made a mental note to ask Abraham about it.

"It's a splendid artefact, like the Czarinas would wear! Those are little pearls? Ah, you know, it's bad luck to accept pearls as a gift, and opal in particular is an omen of tragedy."

"Papa, you don't believe that foolishness, do you?" Alma took off her right glove and tried the ring on each finger. It was loose on her fourth finger. She tried the forefinger. That was a better fit.

"Oh, no, I just find superstition fascinating. But for the sake thereof," he produced a penny from his pocket and tossed it at Alma. It missed her open hand and landed in her lap. "Give that to Michael. If you purchase your pearls, there is no ill fortune."

"That's ridiculous!" Michael chuckled, but took the penny from her anyway. It couldn't hurt anything.

"It may be, but it's fun to be a little ridiculous once in a while, don't you think?"

"Perhaps," he put the penny in his breast pocket, leaned close to Alma, and poked her cheek. "Do I get my present now?"

"Oh, yes! It's in the kitchen, I almost forgot!"

She sprang up and tiptoed away with what speed and stealth that she might with the bulk of her skirts (James had dropped off to sleep sitting on the couch). He wondered how the doctor felt about his daughter in such "impractical" dress.

"And where did she get that lovely dress, sir?" Michael watched that big bow in the back disappear. "Surely you didn't buy it for her."

"Oh, no. Her mother made it for her. She was a seamstress, and may still be, I don't know. By about Alma's age, she was proficient enough to pay her way through a year of college one bodice at a time."

"Is that so?"

"Yes indeed. Made her own wedding dress, too, I remember. It was grey, that's her favourite colour. That's why Alma wanted to make hers, though I don't think she's ever sewn a day in her life except to mend holes and put buttons on."

It seemed so appropriate that such a plain and practical man married a woman whose favourite colour was grey.

"Did you like her dress?"

"I thought the skirt to be a bit excessive. You see, fashionable skirts were much bigger back then, and you could not walk very quickly in them. Really, I think skirts could be done away with entirely, and nothing would change for the worse. Corsets, as well— they strike me as unhygienic, and I believe the natural shape of a woman was not meant to be altered, though Alma and Ellen insist that they don't mind them—"

He stopped when Alma hurried back in with a timidly excited look, holding a tin box.

"I didn't wrap it," she admitted, as he could plainly see. "It took me a long time to make because I wanted it to be perfect!"

"You made me a box!" Michael took it from her and turned it over. The contents rattled inside.

"Excellent craftsmanship, and on such short notice!"

"Open it," she commanded, with her lips taut and quivering.

He lifted the lid and found an assortment of brightly coloured sweets pressed in the shape of flowers and fruits, and the aroma was instantly recognisable.

"Marzipan!" He picked up a little rose and marvelled at it. "This must have taken hours!"

"Blanching and grinding the almonds was most of the work. The rest was easy, but I had to use walnuts as well."

"They look very lo—"

He peered into the box, and saw that underneath the first layer of the sweets was a twisted length of thorny brush, about the size of his little finger.

"You lunatic, you really did it!" Micheal burst into a fit of laughter as he pulled the branch out.

"Well, taste it."

He nibbled the edge of the briar. It tasted about how he expected it to.

"It's a bit dry."

She did not reply, only menacingly shook the tin.

"Alright, alright," he popped the rose into his mouth. It was fresh and melted on his tongue, though it was a little coarse. Regardless, he was thoroughly impressed and delighted. "Well, they both taste as nice as they look!"

"I'm glad, then," now that she saw he enjoyed the gift, Alma arranged herself comfortably on the couch, reclining at a sideways slant like the women of ancient Rome might have done.

Dr. Webb departed from the parlour and bid all one last merry Christmas. James snored away, with his face in the cushioning. Alma turned her hand in the light and continuously admired how the opal sparkled. He'd never seen her so captivated by gems.

"So, does my Alma like her ring?" Michael came close and engulfed her.

"She does."

"Do you think you would like to wear it all the time?"

"I think so, at least as long as I'm not doing work that may damage it."

"And if you had it fixed to fit the right finger, would you accept it as an engagement ring?"

Now she looked straight at him. Direct eye contact was so rare coming from her. It was always striking.

"Sir?"

"I love you, Alma," he drew her completely flush with him, with his lips to her cheek. "I want you to be my wife. Would you marry me?"

Her eyes grew so very large and glassy, and through them, he saw the gears turning rapidly in her brain. Perhaps she thought he was being eccentric, but he'd lived with her for months. Having learned of her passions and her mannerisms, finding enjoyment in all of them, he concluded that their differences were not only tolerable, but perfectly matched. He did not feel he was making a rash decision, but he made hasty attempts to mollify her in case she misconstrued his intentions.

"Not right away… but my mind is made up. I want to marry you."

Michael felt her little heart flutter against his clothes, and he maintained an iron grip on her hands, as if he thought she may try to withdraw. Her silence tormented. He steadied his breath and swallowed hard in an effort to keep down the wine and dessert he'd just had.

"Yes, I'll marry you, Michael."

Her words echoed in his empty skull and vibrated every nerve in his body. He could not shout, as the other inhabitants of the house were asleep, but he gathered her to him and squeezed. She let out a strangled yelp, so he released her.

"Sorry," he held her gently at his side and cautioned leaning his head on her bare chest to hear her heartbeat. She did not protest. Though his head spun, he tried to speak calmly and firmly. "I suppose I will soon have to make many preparations, now."

"As will I, sir."

"Alma, you injure me when you do not use my name," he bent his neck so that his brow brushed against the black velvet. "You will soon be my wife."

"Michael," she began slowly. "From now on, I will call you what you wish when we are alone, but in the presence of others, I would like us to behave as we always have; I think it is proper, given your station and mine."

"What do you mean by that?"

"Are you not a gentleman, sir: a nobleman at that?"

That, he was… he'd nearly forgotten.

"As of now, it means nothing. But when we are with company, you may conduct yourself as you please."

"That is well," she smoothed his hair away from his face and kissed his forehead. "But I think I shall go to bed now."

She picked up her gloves and the wrappings, and moved his tin of sweets out of the way.

"May I lie in bed with you for a little while?"

"No, Michael."

"Hmph! You think my intentions are impure?"

"No. But I like my bed to myself, and I will not put temptation in front of you, whatever your intentions are."

"Instead, will you let me have one of your gloves?"

"What for?"

"I think its fragrance would sustain me well enough."

"Fine," she handed him the left glove. "Do not shed the velvet."

"And let me have a kiss before you go?" Michael took her waist and coaxed her closer, leaving a trail of kisses from her forehead, to her lips. It was difficult to do while standing upright. Compared to him, she was miniscule.

"Goodnight, Michael," Alma left the door open behind her.

James was still asleep on the couch. Would he catch a cold sleeping out here? Michael did not really want to wake him, so he draped the blanket over him before he put out the fire.

He lay in bed, turning the penny in one hand and stroking the glove with the other. The coin went on his bedside table. The glove, he set on his pillow, and he turned his face to it as he drifted off to sleep.

He'd had mixed feelings about this Christmas, and a hard handful of months leading up to it, but perhaps these were only the labour pains before a new joy could be born into his life. He even felt inclined to pray over his hopes and his gratitude.

XIII

That morning, he found himself burning with confidence, and sober with peace of mind. Alma was making breakfast, and Dr. Webb was the first at the table. Michael stood before him and held out his hand.

"Sir, I am betrothed to Alma. She has agreed to marry me, and I will direct my efforts towards making a home for her, and making her every bit as happy as I feel in her presence."

Not once did he stop and consider that he should ask, beg, or kiss his feet, because he was stating exactly how things were.

Alma turned and watched the two of them, with her spoon suspended over a pan of crackling ham.

The doctor firmly grasped his hand, with a calm and passive look.

"Well, thank you for telling me that, son. Good luck to you, then."

His workload was very light that morning. He only had mail to take to post, that was all; this meant there was plenty of time to take Alma out to the next village and find a jeweller.

Michael thanked her for breakfast and asked her to be ready to leave with him when he returned.

He'd never ventured out with such a spring in his step before. The streets were glossy and slick with a thin sheet of ice, but he tread as lightly as a little songbird, whistling a nonsense tune as he went about his business.

Everything was beautiful and fresh to his delighted senses. Even Ida was a joy to behold, though her face was pinched into a petulant glare as always, and she was readily advancing to pester him.

"Why do you look that way? What are you so happy about?"

"Ida, you little rat!" Michael took her hands and pulled her into a little twirl.

"Oy, you rake!" she screeched. "I already got me a man, so step off, you hear?"

"A man? Don't make me laugh; you probably don't even understand any of what you just said! So what little delinquent have you cast an unholy spell on? Who's your partner in crime?"

"I can't tell you that! It's a secret!" she stuck her tongue out.

"Fine, keep your secrets. Your confidence is of no use to me, anyway. But since you caught me in such a good mood," he took the penny from last night and tossed it up. "Merry Christmas."

He turned and headed for the post office as she scurried to pick the coin up off the pavement. An odd feeling quelled within him from her words. They did not sound natural coming out of her mouth, because though it was just childish babble, she did not seem to be at an age where she'd be preoccupied with anything resembling romance. She didn't even seem to have any friends.

And why did it concern him?

Michael posted the letter and hurried back to retrieve Alma. He was surprised when he entered the hall and found almost the exact same dress as last night, but with long sleeves and a high collar. She wore it with her blue kid gloves, and was tying down an ornate straw hat covered with crepe fabric and magpie feathers.

"Mama made two bodices: one for daytime wear, and one for the evening," she explained.

"Can you walk down a rocky street in that skirt?"

"Of course I can, though Papa doesn't think so. The train and overskirt come off."

After walking a little ways, they managed to get a ride to the next village. It was in the opposite direction of the abandoned lots, over the train tracks. Though it was smaller, it was newer and more compact, and a lot busier. A street sweeper recognised Alma. She mentioned that Mrs. Webb lived nearby.

"When will I have the pleasure of meeting Alma's Mater?" Michael turned with wicked glee to see her face contort at his wordplay.

"Very soon, I'm sure. But she does not know I haven't contacted any of the suitors she set up for me, and it may be a shock that I've made up my mind to marry a man completely unknown to her. I think I should wait a little while."

"Do you think I would not make a good impression, or perhaps displease her?"

"Not at all, sir. But she is set in her way, and her way only."

"Did she set you up with an upright man of God, ready to make you his missionary wife?"

"No, sir. A solicitor… and a chemist."

"Analytical characters, but probably not suited to your tastes, and unlikely to possess an evangelical heart."

"Unlikely things happen every day. Many people do not know themselves if they are built for the hardships of missionary work."

"I'd think it would be effortless to such a righteous individual."

"Not so, sir. All men falter in righteousness and self restraint, and their mistake is in believing they have mastered it. If it was effortless, more people would practise it."

This was certainly a lot to ponder, and it was difficult to sink into deep thought while avoiding the treacherous puddles crusted with ice. The streets in this town were certainly smoother, but not perfect.

One of his favourite things about Alma was that long stretches without an exchange of words did not trouble her. She filled in the empty space between them with strange tuneless humming. He did not feel pressured to entertain her. Even so, she was always turning to look expectantly up at him, and if he had nothing to say, he simply smiled and tugged at a length of ribbon on her clothes.

She probably would not accept kisses from him on this busy street. Sure, she was all talk about propriety and composure, but he'd seen her with her feet propped on the parlour tables more than once. Sometimes he saw the very tops of her stockings, and a tantalising sliver of white flesh.

Michael found a jeweller willing to adjust the ring, and they agreed on five days to complete the task, but not before the jeweller admired it with a sort of mystified awe, commenting on its exotic peculiarity and unusual gem choice. The rarity of Russian gold led him to charge an extra fee, which Michael begrudgingly consented to.

Wholly against his sense and better judgement, his feet carried him to a textile warehouse where he attempted, once more, to fund Alma's bridal attire. Flustered and frenzied whispers ensued.

"For God's sake, Alma, you will be my bride soon enough!" he hissed. "Let me pay for one little thing, it won't hurt!"

"I could not possibly pay you back."

"You will not ever need to pay me back. Abandon the thought entirely and grab whatever you want."

Somehow the idea of receiving without giving was alien to her, but he waved off her concerns about the expenses because seeing her in her wedding dress would be priceless. Her face glowed with a hot blush as she studied the bolts of fabric, and she seemed a tad bit dejected as she brought him a generous length of floral lace in her shaking hands.

"Did they not have what you wanted?" he took a pinch of the gauzy material and held it up to the light.

"I don't think I'm in a mood for grazing in a warehouse, sir."

"What would you do instead?"

"I would rather be at home."

"So soon?"

"Yes. I am vexed now."

She said this without meeting his eyes, and she walked out with her arms tucked into her cape so that he could not reach for them. Now he himself was put off by the silence.

"Why are you vexed, Alma?"

"You cannot buy my admiration, Michael."

His name on her breath startled him, and the tone made him feel he was being scolded. She continued with her gaze fixed straight ahead.

"I am sure you would soon resent me if you proceed to give so much so early, and so readily."

"Not so!" he exclaimed wildly. The very idea of resenting her was abhorrent to him. "Have you not given me more than anyone would expect of you from the first day? And is that hidden sweetness not what drew me to you before I'd even realised it?"

He reached under her hat to move a strand of hair away from her eyes. They were red and shining.

"You are entirely too fearful, and for no reason," he concluded. "Who speaks to you in such a way, that you are so timid? He'll be picking his teeth up off the pavement if I find him."

Her eyes grew wide in amazement, as expected. That remark startled even him when it escaped his lips, and he shuddered as he heard it.

"Nobody, sir. Consider me especially cautious, and try not to feel injured by that fact."

Whether she was being completely truthful or not, he did not know, but all he could do was trust her. Perhaps she was not yet convinced that his feelings were far more than a childish whim.

And on the subject of childish whims…

"Alma, you would not believe what your little Ida told me earlier today."

"No? What did she say?"

"She told me 'I got me a man, so step off!'" Michael began the account with an attempt at mimicking her piercing voice, the effort of which scraped his throat raw.

Alma gave a titter at his absurd impression, and then the humour dropped from her face in an instant.

"What? Why would she say something like that?"

He explained the exchange in great detail, and ended by asking her if she had heard anything of the sort from Ida herself.

"No indeed!" she scratched aggressively at her chin. "I imagine she picked it up from some women in town and is either telling a tale, or playing a game with one of the boys from school. It's just something childish, I'm sure."

"Well, I should think you ought to talk to her about it yourself," he decided. "Do you not think it will start strange rumours, or even get her into trouble if she spouts nonsense?"

Her brows knit together.

"So perhaps I might worry about the little brat from time to time!" Michael spat. He thought of mentioning that there were already rumours in town circulating about the Webbs, but he decided against it, because she likely either already knew or would be troubled to find out.

He waved down a ride back home, and it was completely dark by the time they reached the house.

Only James was home. He had just come inside from tending to the chickens, and he was not wearing any one of his new hats. Michael decided not to say anything presently and gave Alma all the kisses he'd wanted to give her that afternoon as he took off her hat and cape by the door.

"James!" it seemed she thought it necessary to speak on his behalf. "What about your new hats! I don't think Michael bought them for you just because he thought they'd look nice hanging on the stand!"

James answered with an incoherent string of grumbling and shut himself up in his chamber.

She huffed and unbuttoned her gloves.

"I'll start dinner, then," she said, but she soon scurried over to Sophie's nest to fawn over the new kittens. Michael did not particularly want to see them, but he wanted to see Alma, so he followed her to the nest in the corner. As it was very dimly lit, he could only see the vague outline of their little wriggling bodies as they squealed. Knowing her so well, it likely took a great deal of self restraint to abstain from picking them up.

"Well, they'll be opening their eyes soon," Alma declared as she stood up and smoothed her dress, realising just now that she had not changed into appropriate attire, and retreated to her room.

Michael stood at her threshold and listened to her disjointed humming. She came out in her grey work dress. As backwards and ludicrous as it seemed, he almost preferred the plain clothes to her lovely red dress. He could place a hand on her neck or her waist without worrying about mashing a standing crop of lace and incurring her wrath. It was also a far less complex arrangement; the fewer layers concealing her shape, the better.

"Ah, Michael, what do you think you would like for dinner?" she came upon him with an enthusiasm he did not anticipate and hid her face in his jacket.

"Anything you cook would be just fine."

"I found half of a dead mouse in the cellar this morning. Wouldn't want to waste it."

"Delicious. Carrots would do nicely on the side."

Michael reclined on the floor of his room, nibbling marzipan and grazing over a dreadfully dull book on taxes and finances. This all would have been useful to know before selling his property. His father had thought to personally tutor him in English, French, and German, but never once taught him anything about money.

Still, he tenderly brushed his fingers over the old silk handkerchief on his neck. This one still smelled of his acrid pomade… Michael did not part out his hair and comb it flat as his father did, though Abraham insisted.

"While handsome fellows are moulded of fine marble, you are carved from granite!" he once said. "Vanity does not suit you. You are no dandy, and have no need for oiled curls!"

But whether it was fashionable or not, it could not be helped. He had his mother's hair, and his sister also had a few dark ringlets…

He thought of her frozen for all eternity in a still and faded image, and he slammed the book shut and stepped into the hallway.

Alma was, in fact, preparing carrots, but no mouse. Instead, there was stewed rabbit and potatoes, the remnants of Christmas dinner. In typical Alma Webb fashion, it was all mashed together, frying on the stove. It squeaked when she stirred it.

"It's nothing special, since I imagine Papa won't be home until much later," she laid out plates and served tea. "Sit down, then."

She hurried out of the kitchen with a plate of scraps for Sophie. He pulled up a chair, but waited for her to return before he seated himself.

James emerged from his lair.

"Ah, Mr. Webb, how are you getting on this evening?" Michael cautioned to ask.

Again, James mumbled something he could not understand.

"Enunciate, man."

"Hmph," he took his plate from the table and stalked back to his room.

"Same to you."

Michael sat down when he saw Alma again.

"James has learned that you will marry me," she explained. "It is a bit of a shock for him, I suppose."

"He'll get over himself. You are a grown woman."

"So I am," she murmured as if she hardly believed it herself, and clasped her hands in quick prayer over her meal. She'd done it many times before, but he didn't usually take notice of it, because they did not often eat alone and many things competed for his attention. He felt a slight pressure to mimic her.

Dinner, of course, was wonderful, and quite tranquil with just the two of them at the table. Their conversations were never trite and strained. He fancied this was what marriage would be like.

The mundane world that used to gnaw at him was now a pleasant dream. Though he always craved more of it, he enjoyed Alma's company in their leisure time— and the times he hung over her while she worked.

He knew she would soon depart for her formal nurse's training, at the doctor's expense, and in her mother's presence. It would have undoubtedly been improper for Michael to accompany her, but he was still tempted to ask.

Even he was quite busy. Woodwork was not merely a hobby, but the start of a legitimate profession; he was still an apprentice, but he improved steadily. Michael was a tremendous help, as he was strong and nimble, and his master Mr. Liddell was losing steady use of his hands. He went into the shop twice a week.

He had regular work and habits to occupy himself with in the coming year, no longer weighed down by the distant future.

Abraham continued to write, though Michael now had to compose his letters in large print that he could easily read.

James *eventually* began to accept what was what, and Dr. Webb approved of him more each day.

Alma finished her wedding dress. Michael peeked at her wearing it in her room, but of course he didn't tell her. He saw it was a simple and elegant pearly robe with sumptuous draping in the back, but a more orderly and streamlined front. The collar was high, brushing her jaw, and the sleeves were slender.

And yet he saw not one stitch of the lace he had bought for her. What had she done with it?

Still, she was clearly pleased with it, and his heart burst open to see her twirl and sigh at the looking glass. He anticipated seeing how the whole bridal ensemble would come together.

One day…

XIV

After many minutes, she then began to take it off, and he tore his burning face away from the keyhole before he was spotted.

He'd not seen anything that he was not meant to see, but he felt guilty about invading her privacy in that way. He continued to speak of her dress as though he'd never seen it finished, and was prickling with excitement— he truly was, and mentioned it every day.

"Michael, do you not have a birthday approaching in February?" Alma came to him in the parlour after breakfast one morning.

That was right… the twenty-seventh. He had almost forgotten it entirely. He would be twenty in about a month.

Only twenty, and yet he could not stop himself from thinking that he had already wasted his youth. After all, what had he really accomplished? Realistically, what could he *hope* to accomplish?

"So I do. And what of it?"

She knelt on the floor with her laced fingers upon his knee. With the curtains drawn back, she took on the colours of a perfect English winter morning. Her face and hair were freshly fallen snow mingling with the last remnants of autumn leaves, and her eyes were a creek rushing wildly beneath the frozen surface.

"Well… I can't think of what you may want. Is your supply of marzipan dwindling?"

"Don't worry about it. You know I am a simple man. I don't need much."

"I'm not asking you what you *need*. What would you like?"

"To be frank, I didn't want to think much of it, Alma. It's a day like any other, and I intend to treat it as so."

"What is the matter? Why are you so dreary all of a sudden? The prideful Lord Bennett doesn't care for his own birthday?"

"Alma, don't worry about it, I said!" Michael dislodged her fingers from his leg. Hearing his empty title used mockingly really pricked him.

She stared up at him for a moment with one of those unreadable expressions, and then rose up and slowly walked out without a word.

Shame seized him by the throat so that he could not call her back. He hadn't meant to strike her sensitive nerves.

She came back on her own, with a cup of tea that she brought to him. It seemed the river was thawing. Her eyes were shining and wet.

"Alma," he grasped the little hand that placed the tea on the table, and chafed it in his fingers. "If you want, you can cook something special. How about that?"

"Like what?"

"Surprise me."

This clearly irritated her, but it must have been better than brooding over a little slight. She resolved to be content either way.

"Well, I'll do my best," she turned to leave, but he pulled her back.

"You're not gloomy, are you?" Michael tugged at a lock of her hair and brought her face close. He was not very good at apologies.

"I am not. I am easily flustered."

"You are, yes, though nobody would think it by looking at you, I imagine."

"I have work to do, though, and you probably will soon."

"Correct," he kissed her ear. It was the closest to him. "Go on, then."

After having his tea, he set out into town to run his errands (for which he was now being paid only twenty shillings a week, as an incentive for him to acquire another profession; carpentry was slow in winter, but he at least had a solid foothold) and found the streets slick with a thin sheet of ice on the stretches where trees blocked out the sun. This slowed him down significantly. Luckily, as it was a degree warmer that day, the ice wouldn't last long.

The townsfolk were exceptionally warm as well. The clerk at the pharmacy was all smiles and sweetness as he detailed his engagement to his dearest Alma, and she offered him a free bag of peppermint drops when he paid for the tobacco. He did not often eat peppermints, but perhaps others in the house would like them.

A flock of brand new school children marching along the walk marvelled at his size. They wanted to climb him like a tree. As he had somewhere to be, he brushed their pawing fingers off of his coat and nudged them away, taking care not to trample them, as tempting as it was.

One young boy who somehow knew him by name insisted with glee that his father could have most definitely thrashed him good.

And maybe he could have, but as much as he missed the thrill of boxing, he didn't exactly want to find out.

He declined. The boy certainly pressed, though.

"What, are you a chicken? Oy, Bennett's just a big chicken!" he thrust his finger in Michael's face, somehow able to see him under his large floppy hat and wild mess of curls hanging over his eyes.

Perhaps this was Ida's "man." How silly. Michael would interrogate him some other time.

For all their prodding, they scattered when he put up a front as if to chase them. They took to playing on the other side of the street, bothering a pair of old ladies instead of him.

He had a pint of cider after he finished what he needed to do in town, and after a pleasant but largely meaningless confab with Mr. Briggs, he took his time ambling about outside as the sun continued its rapid descent. Lamps were being lit. It was completely dark before long. All those children were hurrying home with their little scarves fluttering in the wind.

All except one…

He'd recognise the voice anywhere. Ida could be heard as a faint echo far back in the alleyway at the edge of town.

He stepped as lightly as he could. Another hushed whisper mingled with hers, but he could not make out any words. She'd probably never been so quiet before in her entire life. What diabolical plot was she carrying out?

He prepared himself for anything— or at least he thought he did.

"Ida!" Michael barked at the two silhouettes crouching in the dark. "What are you doing out so la—"

The streetlights splashed across their faces when he shifted his weight, and the two figures were now plainly visible, their expressions frozen in terror. One was Ida, and the other was Albert Gillman.

"Ida!" he shouted again, snatching her by her arm and rending her from Gillman's side. "What are you doing! Why have you—"

Michael realised his anger was directed at the wrong person. He flung her behind him and lunged forward to detain Gillman as he was trying to make his escape. He let out a strangled yelp like a beaten dog as he was apprehended; he squirmed, but it was futile.

"And what do you want with Ida?" Michael spat through clenched teeth. "She is a child. What do you want with her?"

"What do *you* want with her?" Gillman raised a thin finger at her while she cowered silently behind Michael.

His heartbeat pounded in his ears faster than he could count its throbbing. Indignation had cut off the part of him that could see reason.

"Answer!" Michael shook him violently enough for his head to bob and sway.

"She was afraid to walk home on these streets alone. I was only going to escort her myself."

"And why slither through the shadows?"

"She felt safest that way."

He turned to look at Ida. He grasped her face and made her look at him. Her lips were sealed, but her eyes betrayed a quivering fear that he had never seen before in a child.

Gillman tried to work himself free when Michael's grip briefly began to slacken. He appeared to move towards Ida, and whether he meant to or not was unclear, but Michael's temper was wrought to its limit.

He released Ida and swung at Gillman. She shrieked as a series of blows landed on his pretty face. Pitiful man. He fell like a rotting oak and never put up a fight.

The first strike was for his rage, and the subsequent hits were for the familiar feeling he'd missed. He was maddened and blinded by that feeling.

Ida was hysterical, first pulling at his coat until the sash ripped, and then trying to block his fists. He froze with his hand only an inch away from her face.

Michael's wrath cooled in an instant. He looked down at Gillman. His face was like a smashed tomato, and he was trying fruitlessly to wipe away the blood as it flowed from his nose and teeth. With his coat thrown open, Michael could see the ugly little scarf Ida made was twined round his neck.

Anger rose within him again, but he had greater problems. Ida was sobbing and sputtering still, and it was only a matter of time before somebody came to investigate.

"You—" he cast a hand down at Albert Gillman as if delivering divine judgement. "You stay away from this girl."

Gillman croaked something incomprehensible and began to drag himself away.

"Ida, you're going to Alma and Uncle Webb," Michael seized her hand and tugged, but she would not budge.

"Ida, come."

"No!" suddenly she was combative: twisting, straining, and kicking to extricate herself. "Let me go, you brute!"

"Have it your way, then," he scooped her up and slung her over his shoulder like a sack of potatoes.

She continued kicking and swearing and almost made him drop her for quite a stretch until she eventually resigned to her fate.

"I hate you," she finished her tirade.

"Go ahead. It makes no difference to me. What were you doing with that man? Has he touched you?"

"No! He was my friend and you hurt him!"

"How long has he been your friend?"

"I'm not s'posed to tell."

"Too late for that now, isn't it? Anyway, I'm taking you to Alma and you can tell her all about it."

He threw the front door wide open and deposited a snivelling Ida in the hall.

"Alma, come here now!" Michael called out, taking a handful of Ida's pretty purple coat so that she could not run away.

Alma came downstairs, first looking pleased to see them, and then her look distorted into one of horror and confusion.

"Michael?" she leapt straight over the remaining steps and rushed forward. "What's the matter? What happened to Ida? Why are you all bloody?"

"Just worry about Ida. I found her creeping around in the dark with a mosquito. Examine her."

She did as she was told, but seemed to be struggling to make sense of the scene she had just stumbled upon. Her movements were slow and stiff, and her eyes were unfocused. He'd already locked himself up in his room when she called after him. She did not pursue.

XV

Alone with his thoughts, he was seized by an oppressive feeling of dread as he disrobed and washed the blood on his hands with cold water from the basin. Just now, he began to realise what he'd done.

Gillman's ruined face flashed in the darkness when he blinked. Albert Gillman was a monster. He did not feel remorse for beating him (on the contrary, he felt that his unsavoury presentiments were finally justified) but he could not shake away this new sense of terror that gripped his vitals. He trembled violently, and not from the cold.

Never put up a fight...

The blood wouldn't come out of his coat sleeves. He slathered the cuffs in lye soap and scrubbed with a wire brush until the threads were torn and frayed, but the blood remained. He'd only succeeded in further ruining his coat, and dashed it on the floor in a desperate fit.

Now that the anger and excitement had burned off, his strength betrayed him. He vomited up what little was in his stomach, onto his coat, and sank to the floor with his head spinning and his hands throbbing. Ida was yelling over Alma's fretting and sighing in another room.

The frenzy drew James out of his chamber to question the ladies, but he must have been sent away, because his footsteps promptly returned. Michael was half afraid that he would come pounding on his door next. He waited, but it never happened. He was safe for the moment.

He shut his eyes and stopped his ears. He did not want to think about what had happened. He wanted to wake up and find that none of it was real.

Unfortunately, the putrid stench of blood and vomit and the ache of his bruised knuckles that hit him with the force of a train when he awoke said otherwise.

It was half past seven o'clock. There was a little tap at his door.

"Who is that?" Michael demanded.

"It's Alma."

He did not want to be seen like this, but he could not find the resolve to tidy himself up, either, nor did he want to send her away. Surely, he owed an explanation.

He rose and unlocked the door, trying to ignore the flashes of light swimming in his eyes.

"Come in," he said.

There was a moment of stillness. Right. She'd only ever come into his room to dust and polish while he was away. Inviting her into his chamber was a stepping stone he wished they had crossed over under different circumstances.

She opened the door at last, and she looked as though she had aged thirty years.

"Where is Ida?" he asked, as she was what brought them here to begin with.

"She is sulking upstairs in my mother's old bedroom. Now—"

"What did she say to you?"

"Well, she told me about you thrashing Mr. Gillman… why did you do that?"

"Why! You—" he stopped himself, as it was possible that Ida had not told her the whole truth, or even part of it. He tried to explain as best as he could: "He was lurking in an alleyway with Ida, and he could not give me a clear answer as to what he was doing with her. He even had on a little scarf she had knitted. Of course, Ida surely would not understand the severity of such a situation, so she tried to stop me."

"You should not have done it, Michael."

"Why do you say that?"

"To the best of my knowledge, I determined he has never put his hands on her—"

"So I should have waited until he did?" his voice rose, but not to the point of shouting.

"I'm not saying that! I just feel… " Alma trailed off, and her eyes darted around the room. She continued in a murmur.

"You know it has been rumoured, though he is a university-educated man, that he is quite…

hmm… a dim-witted fellow. It's possible that he did not know what he was doing."

"Obviously he knew he was planning something devious, or he wouldn't have made her keep it a secret! He is a reprobate, dim-wit or not."

"But do you not think you should have just turned him over to the authorities instead?"

"He is—!"

Michael drew in a cool breath to gather himself, then lowered his voice in case people were listening.

"He is the magistrate's dear nephew, Alma. What repercussions do you think would be brought down on him? None, until he actually harmed somebody and the public outcry was too great!"

"That's true, I suppose…"

"You *suppose.*"

"Well, I don't know!" she admitted.

"That's right, you don't. So don't say anything."

Alma gave an unintelligible cry of exasperation and cradled her face in her hands. He saw her eyes wander to his coat.

As impatient as he had become, her distress made him ache. He'd forgotten she needed to be handled with extra care.

"Now, Alma," he pulled her towards him and folded her into his arms. She leaned into him but would not embrace him. "I do have just one favour to ask of you. Have you told James what happened?"

"No."

"That is well. Then do not do so, and I'd ask you not to tell your father, nor let Ida tell anybody. She will listen to you. It would undoubtedly trouble him a great deal, don't you think? Don't bother him with it, alright?"

"I'll do my best."

"Then that is all I shall ask of you," Michael pressed her closer still, and kissed along her most beloved brow. "Oh, and… was there something you wanted to ask?"

"No," Alma pried herself free and slipped behind him, into his room. "I'd just like to clean up your coat. It's been bothering me this whole time."

"You may find it to be a daunting task," he warned her and followed to grab the bloody basin on his toilet table.

"This is nothing. Ida wet the bed until she was eight."

Michael rinsed the basin, then sat in the parlour and waited while Alma washed his coat. Magically, she brought it back spotless, and hung it up by the hearth to dry.

"Well, dinnertime was interrupted. I need to prepare supper now."

"Don't strain yourself. You've done a lot today," he said as he brought his face down for a kiss, but she turned away from him and retreated into the hall.

"Alma!" he came after her and seized her by the sash of her dress. "What about you? Are you alright?"

"I am, sir, or at least I shall be soon."

"Then why will you not kiss me?"

"Your breath is horrid."

He caught a whiff for himself, the impact of which caused him to retch again.

"Oh, that's terrible," he rasped, instantly feeling a twinge of shame for having subjected Alma to his malodorous diatribe.

He washed his mouth out before he came near her again. The stench was gone, but his breath was still perfumed with alcohol. There was not much he could do about that.

Alma was in the kitchen, tending to a chicken roasting in the oven, and a fragrant cabbage soup boiling on the stovetop. She turned to glance at Michael as he shut the door, but quickly snapped her head back.

"Papa is late again," she mumbled and put water on for tea.

"He is, yes. He never does turn down a call at any hour. How is my Alma now?"

"I am much better now, sir," she said, and did indeed sound better…

… though she was back to calling him "sir," even in private. He desperately wanted to ask why, but decided not to, lest he aggravate any sour mood she may have been in. He still wanted that kiss.

Michael sat at the table and just watched her. That, he never grew tired of, and now that he was clean, calm, and collected, he was ravenous. The wonderful smells kept him fixed to his spot.

Dr. Webb arrived just as Alma was carving up the chicken. She apologised for starting supper later than anticipated.

"Oh, don't apologise, Alma. After all, I came home later than anticipated," he chuckled and took a seat across from Michael. "And hallo there, Michael. Are you well? You look a mite dishevelled."

"He'd taken ill earlier this afternoon," said Alma, before Michael was forced to come up with an answer. "I had to wash his coat, so I missed dinner and started supper late. It's drying by the fire."

"Oh! What ails ye, my boy? Perhaps the stew had gone off?"

"If it was the stew, I reckon we'd all be sick, Papa. You know his stomach is easily upset."

"Yes, indeed, but it never hindered his ability to speak as far as I know. Let him answer for himself, Alma."

"I must have had bad ale, sir, but I've finished all of my work for today," Michael straightened himself out in an effort to look somewhat less ragged. "I think I shall feel better after I eat."

"That, you may. Alma's cooking might cure just about anything."

That is, unless Alma's own ailment was the one in need of remedy. The soup was thin and weak in flavour, and the chicken was dry. It was noticeable, but not bothersome. Michael still ate gladly and asked for seconds.

"Oh, Papa, I almost forgot to tell you!" Alma squeaked when the tap of footsteps could be heard from above. "Ida came here today, but she fled upstairs when Michael became ill— why I thought she'd be ill herself! And since it is too dark to send her home now, I figured I would just feed her and put her to bed."

"So that's what that commotion was!" James emerged, having just sat down. "Girls and their faint temperaments…"

Alma curled her lip at his remark as she began to clear the table.

"That's perfectly fine, Alma," Dr. Webb said as he lit his pipe. "No wonder you look so pale and anxious. It sounds to me like you've had quite the afternoon. Has such excitement steered you away from your pursuit of nursing?"

"No. On the contrary, it makes me feel all the more prepared for it. I even think I shall be off for my official training soon."

"Do as you please. I'll accommodate you best I can."

After cleaning the dishes and looking after Sophie, Alma took a bowl of soup upstairs to Ida, and presumably warned her to keep quiet about what she had seen.

Michael was there to greet her at the bottom of the stairs, with his arms outstretched. He received a weak smile and a half-hearted kiss before she retired to her chamber.

It was clear that she did not often lie to her father, if at all. Michael felt poorly of himself for asking her to do such a thing, but it could not be helped. He feared his livelihood would be at risk if Dr. Webb knew what he had done. Though he was a reasonable and understanding man, Michael could imagine he would be somewhat hesitant to keep a violent ruffian under his roof.

Michael remembered similar circumstances, when he was sixteen.

Some young men with fragile egos become enraged when defeated in boxing. It was usually the biggest fellows he fought that took defeat the hardest, thinking their size and strength would carry them effortlessly through a fight.

Once the match was over and he let his guard down, he'd been at the receiving end of retaliation numerous times, in the form of hair pulling, biting, a hard kick to the pelvis, or in one instance, a deep cut on the nape of his neck— the lad insisted that he was going to take his scalp.

The boy's friends who had been restraining Michael released him when they heard that. They said it was too much for them, and they would not allow it. Michael wrestled the knife from his assailant's hands, though not without receiving another slice between his thumb and forefinger.

This was Michael's chance to walk the path of mercy, and forgive.

He did nothing of the sort, and his fellows did nothing to stop Michael from beating the lad into pulp.

"Tell me your name," Michael demanded.

He spat blood in Michael's eye.

Michael struck him once more in the jaw.

"I say, tell me your name!"

"Peterson," he choked.

"Well, Peterson," he threw his bloody knife back to him. "Stay out of my way."

Peterson never bothered Michael again.

He did not feel bad for beating Peterson. Some people did not listen to reason.

But the sensation of having done so was sickening… he remembered the thrill he felt in that moment. It pleased him to make those men bleed, and that frightened him.

XVI

He should not have gone to sleep with those thoughts.

There was a strange mist over the walls of his dream, as if the colours he knew just weren't quite there. He carried a lit candle that produced no light, and he opened the sewing room to find Alma stooped over a broken little body. The young girl had been contorted in a way that he did not think human bones were capable of, and her whole face was red and black with blood. Alma sponged it all away with one swipe, revealing Ida! She grinned, and her lips spanned her whole face. Alma turned to him, with large, glass-like eyes and no mouth, yet her voice said, "look at what you've done."

He tried to speak, but when he parted his lips, he spat out a whole tooth, and then when he checked his mouth, he felt that all of his teeth were loose and crumbling.

He turned to flee from the room, dropping the candle. Immediately, it kindled the drapes in a dull, shadowy flame. Alma snatched at his coat, and he shed it as he escaped.

"Coward! Coward!" James Webb shouted from the top of the blazing staircase, wearing Micael's coat.

He blinked, and then he was watching the house, barn, and trees burn from the street. The only other onlooker was a middle-aged farmer he'd seen many times.

"The oversight concerns me," Michael told him.

"It's done. You killed them."

He swung his fist at the old man, but he was not there anymore, nor was the Webb property. The field was bare, as though nobody had ever lived there. This dark emptiness was more frightening than any other vision. It was thick and heavy, and it woke him from a deep, death-like slumber.

The morning was the same as any other, and yet everything was all wrong.

He went to the parlour to retrieve his coat. It was almost good as new, with even the worried fibres trimmed. Though it was clean and dry, it left a heavy and slimy sensation when he put it on.

Michael continued working as usual. There was not much else he could do, and he had resolved to put the ordeal behind him. Gillman likely would not be bothering Ida anymore.

He did not see much of her at all those next few days. Alma did not divulge any details at what precisely she had told Ida, but expressed her hopes that she would stay in school. If not, she would send her to Mrs. Webb.

Though he tried not to dwell on it, he often found himself thinking about what that wraith might have done if he had managed to lure her away undetected. The very thought curdled his blood and rekindled a passionate rage within him.

He used that fury to fuel the force of his axe as he cut up firewood. It was always relieving and pleasantly mind-numbing to work himself to the edge of exhaustion.

Halfway through his task, he caught a strange feathery mass out the corner of his eye, near the barn. He put down the axe.

Upon closer inspection, he determined it was one of the chickens, most certainly dead, having likely frozen. It was not significantly decomposed, nor did it have any visible wounds. He was never friends with the chickens (and yes, he ate poultry quite often) but he could not help feeling a bit sad and disturbed, gazing at its pallid corpse.

Alma did not need to see it. Michael went straight to James to tell him about it. At first, he did not believe him because he insisted he knew for a fact he had shut them all up securely, so it must have belonged to someone else. He eventually managed to coax him outside to investigate.

"You recognise that bird?" Michael pointed it out to him.

James studied its markings, and let out a disappointed sigh.

"Damn, I thought I'd closed them all in before the cold snap," he said as he tugged at his whiskers, displaying more emotion than Michael had ever heard from his gruff monotone. "It must have wandered off— God, poor thing."

"Honest mistake, man," Michael tapped him on the shoulder. "We'd better hurry up and get rid of it before Alma comes out and finds it."

Luckily, James elected to do it himself. Michael did not want to pick it up, but would not put his manhood on the chopping block by saying that aloud. James went away to fetch the means to do so, still mumbling that he definitely thought he counted the chickens. Michael understood what it was like to brood over such a blunder.

Of course, he still told Alma that one of the chickens had died. She huffed and wrung her hands about it for a while, but ultimately accepted it, saying she knew it was bound to happen from time to time, especially since winter days were so dark.

Alma had retreated into her studies as of late. They now only held private congress for very few precious minutes in the evening, and it was during these past few days that he pined for her attention most of all. He anticipated the next Sunday, when she would not be so busy.

And that Sunday was an agonising slog. He did not appear at church that day, as he felt sick from his nerves. He loathed the feeling of rotting away in bed late into the morning, but he could not summon the resolve to get up. Alma brought toast and tea to his bedside table before she left. He never took one bite, and tore it to shreds for the chickens.

Seeing her come home was a blissful rapture that pulled him out of his brooding!

Only for her to repair to her room until dinnertime. While she tended to the Sunday roast, she clearly did not want to be molested, so he occupied himself on the piano.

At least he was able to coax some insignificant talk out of her at the table. Dr. Webb behaved no differently. He assumed that her agitation was due to her apprehension about going to London.

After the meal, Michael entered the parlour and found her reading her bible as usual, with a handful of tiny kittens wrestling and wriggling in her lap. They finally resembled cats.

"Al-ma, my Alma," he cooed and scooped the kittens out of her lap. If he had been feeling reckless, he could have fit them all into one hand. They swayed and struggled to regain their footing, curiously sniffing this new terrain. One of them tried to hiss at him, but it came out as a little puff.

"Would you read to me again?" Michael set them to one side on the couch, then placed Alma onto his knee and put the kittens back in her lap.

She adjusted the kittens and turned to a new page, then she began to read. He was not well-versed in the Bible, but he fancied she was reading from one of the four gospels. Her voice always set him at ease, and it breathed life into the archaic, florid language of the scripture.

He listened passively, with his face in her hair. The kittens decided he was something to play with. He wrestled them with only a few fingers; their little teeth and claws did no harm to him. It tickled him to take their tiny feet in his thumb and forefinger. He shook them, formally introducing himself.

Nothing that she was reading jumped out at him until she reached the arresting of Jesus Christ. Her words swelled around him as she recited:

"'... for all they that take the sword shall perish with the sword.'"

"Ho!" he stopped her and looked over her shoulder at the words on the page. "What is that you are reading?"

Alma cast a startled look back at him.

"It's the Gospel of Matthew. What's wrong with it?"

She looked completely innocent and confused; so it was not likely that she meant to indirectly provoke or condemn him with the passage she chose.

"Hmph... " he wiped his palms on his trousers. "Nothing. Proceed."

Michael lapsed back into his languid state as she read. Sophie's soft cries emerged from the doorway, and she came and took the kittens from him one by one. The third, second to last, needed its claws carefully dislodged from Alma's gown. Michael tried to reach for Sophie, but she slighted him, and he only caught the end of her plume tail. She had grown much more reserved as a mother.

Alma's fragrance lulled him into a dream. Her skin was smooth as warm butter when he ran his lips over her neck. He found his way to her ear and took just the corner in his teeth.

She tensed up and stopped reading, which shook him from his stupor.

"Don't caress me. I am not in that sort of mood at the moment," she readjusted herself against him and continued reading.

Now unsure of what to do with his hands, he began plucking at the little ends of threads on his coat, which was something Abraham constantly scolded him for as a young boy, but the temptation was too great.

"What are you still tensed up for?" he grasped her taut shoulders, but did not let his hands wander. "And you're so warm. Do you have a fever?"

"I have had a long week. I have not gotten a chance to relax until now."

"Relax now, then," he tugged a little bit to get her to recline against him.

She shut her bible and put it on the side table, then stood up and brushed off her gown.

"No, come back!" Michael whined and pawed at her skirt.

"I'm just stoking the fire, blockhead," she approached the hearth and stoked the flames, as she'd said. Then there was more light.

"Ah, all the better to see you with," he spread his arms and beckoned for her to return.

She curled up against him with her head upon his shoulder. Her breath tickled his neck.

"Well, what sort of mood are you in?" he enveloped her into his coat.

"A pensive one, I think."

"Will you tell me what you are thinking?"

"I won't trouble you."

"Trouble me, Alma."

"I just feel such dread, and I can't shake it off. It's been bothering me for days, and even when I pray about it, I feel vague and uncertain. I don't know what it means."

She clung tightly to his neck as she said this, as if hoping he would sweep her up and carry her to safety.

If he could have, he would have done so.

Her unrest was palpable; her hands were icy cold, and sweat glistened on her face. In truth, he often felt the same, but he was not sure if it was wise to tell her. He had to put up a stalwart facade for her to lean upon.

"Well, you certainly have a lot ahead of you in your future!" Michael produced a handkerchief from his pocket and dabbed at her hot brow. "Going to London and meeting so many new people! It is natural to feel nervous, even fearful."

"But it is not like that," she made herself very small and disappeared into his coat. "It is so cold. I don't feel good or even benign things in my future."

"Am I in your future?"

"Even you feel uncertain and intangible to me," she trembled.

He lifted her face out of his coat so that he could see her, and she could see him.

"On the contrary, nothing in your future is more certain and more close at hand than me. Ah! Is that where the issue lies? Are you nervous about being my bride and stepping into a new sphere of existence?"

"No. That is quite far off, and I feel that danger is upon us even now."

"And is it?" he pressed his forehead onto hers. "Alma, you are safe, and if I need to stand guard at your chamber door all night, then I shall."

"No, that is not necessary. Only promise me that you will be here when I come back."

"Not only will I be here, but I will certainly come straight to you if you need me for anything at all," he smoothed her hair and kissed the bridge of her nose. "Your nerves are strung to their limit, and your stress is manifesting as hypochondria. Get some rest."

She reclined upon him for many minutes, and he allowed himself to be at ease in that interval, but as soon as she left him alone in the dark, his heart began to race against rational thought.

He soothed himself by tapping at Alma's door and seeing that she was secure. Her soft, "yes, I am alright," was sufficient assurance.

Michael went to his own room and sat quietly. Something possessed him to check the windows. He held his breath and heard nothing, so he shut the curtains and lay himself down. Making his rounds in the bedroom set him at ease.

XVII

His first tranquil slumber in many days was shattered by an awful shriek.

He was on his feet, holding his rifle in a matter of seconds. There was a great commotion outside, and a dazzling red light shining through his window. Sunrise, already?

No, a fire.

When he threw open the side door, the air was thick with smoke rushing in. He could scarcely see anything but a monstrous funnel of roaring flames that consumed the barn. It was so deadly hot that he could not feel the chill of the night air.

Townsfolk had gathered in the field to witness the blaze. Some shouted and clamoured. Others gazed as if under a spell. Very few acted.

The Webb men stumbled out, Dr. Webb still putting on his eyeglasses, both looking on in mute, frozen terror that Michael had never seen before.

Alma flew out of the house with her night clothes and loose hair, screaming things Michael could not understand. He intercepted her before she could reach the barn and caught hold of her.

"Michael!" she screeched right into his ear and fought him assiduously. He had much ado to restrain her without injuring her. It was easier once he got ahold of her arms. "Michael, the animals! The animals are in there! Let me go!"

"No! If they can get out, they will, and if not, you'd fry in there!"

She let out a chilling wail as if she really was being burned, but he would not release her.

She continued to fight and struggle as more and more people gathered to be useless onlookers. By the time the fire engine came bowling down the street, all they could do was keep the flames from spreading to the house while they burned themselves out. He did not see even one creature dart out of the building.

It was a terrible and helpless feeling, watching the fire and being unable to act, but he was grave and composed. The best he could do was protect Alma. He gathered her up and carried her away from the smoke. Eventually, she stopped fighting him and went limp in a weeping mess upon his breast.

By the time the sun started to rise, the barn was reduced to a charred frame. It was noticeably cold now, and Dr. Webb brought coffee out to the volunteers and examined mild injuries. People stared and talked amongst themselves.

For some reason, it made his blood boil.

"What! What are you looking at? Go home, all of you!" Michael barked at them.

The mob dwindled slowly. Alma had either fallen asleep or fainted. She was cold to the touch, so he brought her inside and made up a fire while she awoke on the couch, swaddled up in all of the blankets he could find.

He expected tears and upbraiding when she sobered up, but she only stared vacantly into the fire. At least the colour had returned to her face, but it was still worrying that she would not speak on her own accord.

"Alma?" Michael replaced the blankets she had shed and chafed her frigid hands. "Alma, it's alright. Can you hear me?"

"Michael, let her be," Dr. Webb called to him as he passed, sounding just as collected as always, but clearly fatigued and shaken. "Do not molest her. She has had quite a shock— we all have, I'd say."

He left her, reluctantly, and went to the doctor to see if he knew anything at all about what had happened.

Dr. Webb and his son were both seated in the kitchen, with untouched coffee mugs at hand.

"What do you think started the fire?" Michael asked.

The elder Webb spread his palms up, as he often did when placed in a difficult situation.

"There was no evidence that it spread from outside, and no electricity runs to the barn. The best explanation anybody could come up with was that hot oil had dripped from a lantern and slowly kindled the old straw."

"But when I examined the remains," added James. "There were burned up bits of twine that I'd never seen, as if the doors had been corded shut."

"Corded shut?" Michael remembered how he saw no animals escape the fire, and his heart dropped. "Why would anyone do something like that?"

"It passes me. We'll deal with that later. James and I will go out and bury all that's left that hasn't been fully burned— before Alma can see it. Michael, I'd like you to head into town and fetch us more coffee, please, and some sugar."

"Yes, of course," he was about to run straight out the door, but then he looked down and realised he was not dressed for the occasion. "Erh, after I make myself presentable."

He shed his besmirched bedclothes and called out to Alma that he would be back as soon as possible. No answer.

On the streets, it was a typical Monday morning, save for the light haze of white smoke, almost like fog. In the shops, folks had formed a body in a corner and spoke in hushed tones amongst themselves. Michael could understand only a little.

"Very strange, indeed."

"Seems none of the animals survived."

"As if they'd been trapped."

"A grudge?"

"Divine retribution…"

"Grudge! *Divine retribution!*" Michael spun on his heel and sprang upon the crowd in a fitful passion. "What are you saying! A just God, if there be one, would not retaliate against the Webbs when there is genuine evil in the world—on these very streets! And what heinous sins could they have committed? None! They would not even speak ill of their fellow man, and there *you* are!" thrusting an accusing finger at them. "Have you not one shred of—"

"Sir! Ah, young man!" the clerk waved him down from behind the counter. "I will have no disturbances, please. Either purchase something, or save your sermon for Sunday."

He was still livid, but he agreed to be just civil enough to buy what he wanted and leave without a fuss. His head reeled from what he had heard, and he was acutely aware of the whispers now directed at him as well.

All he knew was that he could no longer ignore these rumours about Dr. Webb, if there was even the smallest prospect of that fire being connected, and putting everyone in danger.

There was a second possibility fluttering at the back of his mind, but he shut it out, as it was too dreadful to consider.

Mr. Briggs, at least, voiced some semblance of genuine concern when he passed by.

"Bennett!" he called from the steps of his
establishment, running a hand through his
greying, feathery hair. "There you are! I hear the
Webbs' barn burnt up to cinders, and they saw
the smoke for miles around! I come back from a
weekend's holiday, and I hear all over town! I
say, every time I leave and come back, there's
something amiss!"

... every time?

"'Tis true, Mr. Briggs," Michael answered. "Total
loss, and all the animals were trapped. Happened
early this morning."

"Oh, how terrible! Give me regards to the
doctor, ol' boy. And do come round any time to
tell me all about it."

Typical Mr. Briggs. He loved visitors. It was
probably an essential trait when one spends his
days pouring whiskey for lonely men to drown
their sorrows in.

On his way back, he saw Ida going the same
way as him, walking with a determined gait.

"You there!" he shouted and crossed the street to
intercept her. "Do I need to tell Alma you've
been dodging school?"

"How can I sit in school?" Ida marched on without even turning to look back at him, so she must have been in a serious state of mind for once. "Alma must be so distraught. She needs me."

Only your own mother could find solace in your company, he was tempted to say, but given what he'd heard about her mother, he kept it to himself.

"Just like you to use your poor cousin as an excuse to stay out of school! Well, don't prod her, and behave yourself! She is in no condition to fret over you."

"I'm always on my best behaviour!"

"Then I'd truly hate to see you at your worst."

"Oh, what's in that parcel?" she asked, possessing the mind of a squirrel, as always.

"It's coffee. You wouldn't like it."

"I might. Could I taste it?"

"At the peril of your life! I imagine your little head would burst, and we've enough messes to worry about as of late."

From the stile, he could see the remains of the barn, looming in its shadow as a ghostly reminder of last night's disaster. A disturbed plot of soil on one side of the field marked the mass grave.

It seemed all of the soul had been sapped from the home, and time itself had stopped. All was still and silent inside. Nobody was in the kitchen when he stored the coffee.

"Alma? Doctor or Mr. Webb?" Michael stuck his head into each room he passed, searching for any signs of life. Ida ran straight to Alma's room and let herself in. Sophie and the kittens were nowhere to be found. Surely Alma had just taken them into her room with her.

He really ached to speak to her, but hopefully Ida was enough of a comfort until she decided to come out.

The telltale scent of burning blackberry tobacco told Michael that Dr. Webb was in his study upstairs. The door was left ajar, so he took the liberty of leaning into the doorway. He had not been there in quite a while, and he was pleased to see that his shelf was being put to good use, but he had more pressing issues to discuss than the furniture.

"Dr. Webb, sir," he addressed him as he crossed the threshold.

The old man had his elbows on the table, with his face in one hand, and his pipe in the other.

"Greetings, Michael," the doctor said without looking up, which was incredibly unusual for him. "Have a seat if you'd like."

"Thank you, sir," he sat directly across the desk. "I really am sorry about the barn. Perhaps if I had awoken earlier—"

"No, no, you needn't apologise. Even if you'd gotten there just as the blaze started, you could not contain the fire on your own, and help would have arrived much too late… " he paused to take a long draught of his pipe, and continued. "You know, that sort of thing is the reason I took my practice to the country."

"I thought you just hated the city."

"Ah, that, too. There was good money to be made, being a private physician to wealthy folk in the city, but I believe the open country is a more suitable environment to rear children. Anyway… a good friend of mine from way back when I was about your age— when Rome was the reigning empire—" he chuckled and coughed into his hand. "She never left the countryside way up north. I continued to write her every so often. Well, some twenty or so years ago, I received the most horrible news. Her first child was due to be born soon, but her labour was complicated, and there was no doctor nearby. By the time help arrived, she had already passed away and delivered a stillborn boy…"

He heaved a rattling sigh and set down his finished pipe.

"It was chilling news, especially so soon after James's birth. Her husband was an upright and dutiful man, ten years her senior. But her death and the loss of the child had demolished him. I'm told he quickly turned to liquor and self-abandon, and died within a year of the tragedy… an entire family, dissolved… I always thought, maybe if somebody had come even an hour earlier…"

Michael said nothing, because he could not think of anything that would alleviate that burden. Instead, he reached over and grasped his empty hand. Now, he was not even sure if he had the willpower to interrogate him.

Still, if somebody really was plotting against them, Michael felt he should warn him.

"But as of now," Dr. Webb rubbed his forehead with his other hand. "The cost of the barn, the chickens, and all that was stored up in there, as well as the damage to the house, will take a substantial amount from my savings. I've been thinking about that all morning, but please don't tell Alma."

"You should have more faith in her capabilities, sir. She can handle much more than she is credited with."

"Oh yes, that is true. But I fear I may need to put off the repairs in order to send her to London as she wishes. If she knew this, I'm sure she would not go."

Slowly, very slowly, Michael released the doctor's hand and reached into his coat, where he still had his chequebook and pencil. With great pains and in stilted, shuddering movements, before he could change his mind, he scribbled a cheque for eight hundred pounds and handed it to Dr. Webb.

The doctor took the powerful note in both of his hands and seemed to read it many times before handing it back.

"Michael, I cannot accept this!"

"You can," Michael assured him. "And you shall."

"I don't know when I'd be able to pay you back."

"Ha! Now I see where Alma gets it. I couldn't possibly hold onto such a fortune, knowing you would be forced to choose between Alma fulfilling her dreams and recovering the losses from the fire."

Henry Webb would not move on his own, so Michael placed the cheque into his hands himself.

After a minute of stillness, he huffed and clamped a hand over his mouth.

"Well, I don't know what to say, Michael."

"Nothing to Alma, that's for sure," he cleared his throat and slipped his chequebook back into his pocket.

"Mr. Bennett, you truly have your father's heart," Dr. Webb continued looking over the cheque as though he could not believe it was real. "It was always his manner to give freely and rejoice in doing so."

At the detriment of his own household, Michael said only to himself, but the sentiment was touching nonetheless.

"That is all well, sir, really," he leaned forward, now feeling, quite audaciously, that he was owed a few answers. "But I think you ought to know that I heard some very strange things while I was out in town."

"Strange things?"

"Yes, quite troubling, even."

"Well, I'm listening."

"It is just the gossip of simple folk with nothing better to do with their time, I'm sure, but they spoke amongst themselves in their congregation, and suggested that this morning's crisis was some divine intervention of sorts… as if you had ever done some deed depraved enough to warrant such a thing. Don't you think it is foolish? As if they had the right to throw any stones!"

All of the peace and rapture had fallen from the good doctor's face, and now his brow was etched with some sort of grief.

"Surely a few souls are only bitter about you leaving the ministry," Michael continued. "You know how the older folks are, when they feel their religion has been slighted, right?"

He did not reply for quite some time, only aged rapidly before Michael's very eyes, and now he was restless with worry.

"Right?"

He set the cheque down on the table and laced his fingers together.

"Goodness, I suppose I owe you an explanation at the very least," he murmured. "Well, I should perhaps tell you why I left the ministry."

"Go on, then."

"I am an adulterer, Michael."

That was a blow that he was glad he was sitting down for. Again, he found himself unable to speak.

"Thirteen years ago," Dr. Webb went on. "I told you that my wanderlust had been sated long ago, but that is not entirely true. Ten years into my marriage, my quiet life, I desperately sought excitement and stimulation. Additionally, I had just given up daytime drinking at the request of Mrs. Webb. Well, a young woman had taken a liking to me. It was quite a rejuvenating feeling that I fought to subdue, but I stumbled… no, I did not stumble— I made an active decision… continuously. I had the convenience of citing house calls as an excuse to take leave, and I lived that way for six months. My relationship with my wife had grown quite strained in the meantime. Not that I can justify my actions in any way. I know I have crossed a line that I can never return from."

Michael found the will to speak at last.

"And you were found out?"

"I was exposed by my own tell-tale heart. Eventually, I felt I could not hide from my sins any longer, and I addressed my congregation at the church on my last day in service. I felt I would be an awful hypocrite if I continued to preach, so I stepped down willingly, and to this day I have not disclosed the name of my mistress, nor spoken to her again. I hope she is well."

The gears started turning in his head… thirteen years ago now… Ida was now almost twelve as far as he knew, and allegedly her father had passed away. Dr. Webb seemed quite invested in her as well…

"Sir, is Ida…" he faltered, because he couldn't believe what he was suggesting.

"Oh, no! No, son, she is not mine. The woman was no relation to the family, but I have sinned nonetheless. And Mrs. Webb… it is true that we often quarrelled over insignificant things, but my treachery was what finally drove her from the home. I offered to leave myself and let her have the house, but she wanted to wash her hands of my sullied reputation and left town altogether, on her own accord. We have been legally separated for eleven years since. And the way my children looked at me when I made that confession… especially James…"

He let his head fall into his hands.

"But I am not looking for you to feel sympathy for me. I am sure that you think poorly of me, and rightfully so."

"I don't think I like you quite as much as I did about five minutes ago, sir," Michael admitted. "But I harbour no feelings of ill will towards you, and that was years ago. Surely not even the most zealous of people would hold it against you still."

"They may, and it is their right to do so. They must feel personally betrayed by their old shepherd."

"Well, what now?" again, he felt bold enough to ask such flippant questions. "If you feel you can not reconcile with Mrs. Webb, would you pursue romance elsewhere?"

After all, you have already committed adultery, he once again thought but kept to himself.

"I could not," Dr. Webb shook his head. "She can if she so desires, but as it stands, she is still my wife, and I will never tarnish my marriage, never again. If I submit myself to solitude, maybe I will finally atone."

"Sir, ask God for forgiveness and atonement, if you believe still."

The irony of him steering the minister towards salvation was not lost on Michael, and it drew an acrid, painful smile from his own lips.

"I have. I do that every day. But Michael… if there is one more thing you could do for me… do not treat my Alma the same way I have treated my wife."

"I would not dream of it sir, but I am sure you did not set out to intentionally injure Mrs. Webb."

"No, indeed. And that is why sin is so treacherous. You never intend to harm anyone, and though you know it is wrong, you find yourself justifying your thoughts, and then your actions more and more, and you are ensnared before you know it. I would tell you not to even allow yourself to be tempted. Do not play with fire."

"Ah, about playing with fire…" Michael pointed in the direction of where the barn once stood. "Do you think anybody here would be spiteful enough to plot against you after all these years? Um… Mrs. Webb, perhaps?"

"Certainly not Mrs. Webb!" the doctor's voice rose sharply, much to Michael's surprise, as he had been so meek and solemn up until this point. "No matter how she may feel towards me, she would not put James and Alma in danger, not ever."

"Of course, sir. That was quite presumptuous of me; I apologise."

"Well… " he combed a hand through his beard as he mused aloud. "Even if the fire was intentional —which I'd hate to assume it was— I cannot for the life of me think of anybody who'd be driven to start it. Did you see or hear anybody behaving strangely?"

"No, sir, not that I remember. I'll definitely tell you if I know anything."

"Thank you very much, Michael, for everything, really. I won't keep you any longer. Why don't you go look in on Alma and Ida?"

"Yes, sir, I think I will," he rose up and departed from the study, shutting the door behind him.

Now he reflected once more on the eight-hundred pounds he had just parted with. The transaction made him feel many confusing things at once; he felt sick, and a little resentful, which he spited himself for, but he also felt happy. Yes, he was so happy. It pleased him to repay the kindness of his benefactor and secure Alma's future. She was *his* future. Besides, it was not a setback he wouldn't be able to recover from.

If even righteous men were subject to temptation, then he did not have to be so critical of his conflicting feelings. He told himself all of this until he felt he believed it, and then he was content. It could not be undone.

However, he was obviously not truthful when he said he would relay all that he knew to the doctor. Foul play could not be confirmed, but it could not be ruled out, either. That night when he confronted Albert Gillman continued to flash in the back of his head. Surely if anybody thought to retaliate for it, they would not make such a convoluted and indirect attack. For now, it was an isolated incident, and still he made an effort to carry on as normal.

XVIII

He guessed it was about noon. Alma and Ida were at the kitchen table, and it pleased him to see her out and about with a smile on her face. Freshly brewed coffee perfumed the air. Even that delighted him until he saw that Ida was given her own cup.

"Oh, Alma, oh no!" Michael rushed down into the kitchen. "What are you doing? Ida doesn't need caffeine, she'll be ricocheting off of the ceiling!"

"You liar!" Ida wrinkled her nose at him. "Alma put milk and honey and cinnamon in my cup, and it tastes just fine!"

"Of course it tastes fine once you add to it until it doesn't taste like coffee anymore," he said as he took a seat across from her: a mistake on his part, as she kept kicking him whilst swinging her legs around, but he was closest to Alma this way. "Though it's probably for the best that you diluted it."

"Neither of you is correct," Alma declared. "It is fine just the way it is, and needs nothing added to it, except maybe a bit of milk to cool it quickly."

"Then let Ida taste from your cup, and see what she thinks of it."

Alma scooted her mug over to Ida, who smelled it first and then took a cautious sip, upon which her face immediately scrunched into a prune. Michael could not contain his laughter.

"Uck!" she shuddered and bore her stained tongue. Then she took another sip and curled her lip again.

"Well, stop drinking it if you don't like it, simpleton!"

"I haven't decided yet," Ida obnoxiously smacked her lips and rolled her eyes into the back of her head.

Michael was told that Ida was not the doctor's child, but he still found himself studying her very closely to find a resemblance. She did possess a likeness to Alma in the teeth and forehead, for instance, but they shared blood on the maternal side. Ida and Dr. Webb both had soft greenish eyes, but in different hues. Alma's were a striking dark blue, almost grey, with flecks of amber that she shared with her father. Michael would just have to take his word for it.

Currently, he was nervous about what might happen when the coffee fully mixed with Ida's blood, but he also wanted to talk to Alma. Visibly, she was well, but it could be difficult to tell with her. They finally had a moment alone when Ida ran off to play with Sophie with a bundle of feathers tied to one end of a string; Alma gave her a stern warning about being careful and watchful of the kittens before she ran off.

"Now, Alma, how do you feel? Are you alright?" Michael drew his chair closer and reached out his hands for her to take.

"I am… managing myself," she lightly placed her hands on his.

"I suppose that is all we can do," he agreed, as even he was hesitant to say that he was well. "I am sorry, Alma. There was really nothing you could have do—"

"I know that."

"I guess you don't need to hear about it… think instead of London. You will be starting a new chapter of your life soon."

"I don't know if I can think about it now. I doubt Papa has the means to pay for both the repairs and my stay."

"Don't worry about it. I spoke to him, and he has it all taken care of."

Or rather, *he* had it taken care of. And he was still coming to terms with it. He was reminded of it again when he adjusted his tie and remembered that it was one of his father's fine silk handkerchiefs he was wearing.

Obviously, he could not hold this against Alma. She did not even know of his decision, and he didn't want her to. He excused himself to go brood about it while she finished her coffee.

Ida's little shoes went tapping all through the hall, punctuated by shrieks as she was chased by a herd of wobbling kittens. Even Alma's titters could be heard once in a while.

And Michael was alone in the parlour, contemplating how fortune had outmanoeuvred him yet again. And why him? What crime had he committed?

Eight hundred pounds; at that moment, it felt so easy and genial to part ways with it, but now it lay heavy upon him, and so did the two thousand pounds he'd refused from Abraham (though the old man would have surrendered it in a heartbeat, Michael would not dare ask him for one penny; he was firm on that).

It would take years to make that back. He tried to run the numbers through his head, and he thought long and hard about any other ways he could earn money. He had yet to gain a footing in carpentry. Boxing was still an option. His face was ruined already, anyway.

The alternative train of thought was abhorrent: unthinkable, even.

The door opened and shut. It was Alma. He did not turn to look at her, but he recognised the footsteps.

She sat behind him (he faced away from the door) and simply rested her hands upon his back, then her head. Unforeseen touches should have delighted him, but in his horribly gloomy state, he found them intolerable.

"Alma," he shook her off. "I'm very busy."

What a stupid thing to say.

"Doing what?" She came to the front of him and tried to take his hands.

"I'm thinking, that's all."

"Thinking about what? You can tell me, can't you?"

"You wouldn't understand."

She scowled and left his side, but came back with a book in hand.

"What about it?" Michael took it but didn't read the title.

"Reading might help you relax."

"I don't need to relax. That won't fix anything."

"Neither will brooding in the parlour," she took a seat across from him and propped her feet up onto the armrest. "Perhaps you'd like me to read to you instead? If you have some time to think—"

"That will do even less! Alma, just don't bother! You're not helping at all!"

He rose from his seat and looked down at her, but it was as if somebody else was in control of his body, and he was only watching.

She said nothing, only stared up as a deer might when it has found itself cornered. Somehow, it vexed him even more.

"Since you seem to be at a loss for words at the moment, get back to me when you actually have something useful to say."

Alma just looked away from him. Her face was red and wet, shining in the firelight, and her features began to contort.

"Tears again!" he tossed the book onto the table, and crossed the threshold. "You're so predictable."

She was an inwardly passionate creature. He expected her to berate him or push him to the floor. He somewhat wanted her to, but she just stared into the hearth with what could only be described as an utterly defeated expression.

As he closed the door, he heard something crash inside. Well, it wasn't anything of his, he was sure.

He went to "his" room— very little in this world was truly his— just as James was coming out into the hall. Michael shut himself in. Alma did not come after him.

Fully clothed, he threw himself into bed and wondered why he'd said what he did. Alma was not at fault, and he vented his frustration upon her. He scorned her touch even though he craved it, and spurned her presence.

He gazed at the ceiling in some sort of earnest. It offered no answers. He glanced into the looking glass and despised what he saw.

And because he had been awake since midnight, his eyes shut on their own.

Alma came into his room. He heard her softly shut the door and approach his bed, and he was petrified. Though he could not see her, he felt her presence looming over him. He could not react.

"Who is like God?" she asked.

Had she really come upon his bed just to deliver a sermon?

"Why are you come?" Michael asked back at her.

"Were you not yearning for me? Do you have no real love for me now that passion has waned, and the excitement has passed?"

These words chilled him to his bones, and vibrated every nerve he had.

"Of course I do! And my passion has not waned, either. On the contrary, it has only swelled."

He lifted his face from the pillows and raised his hands, but he could not see them. He sank into his mattress like a muddy bog, and the clock on the wall read forty-four and fifteen. He blinked, and the numbers were now broken letters.

This was a dream.

Michael turned and rose above his bed. Now he saw Alma. He reached out and grasped her neck, but his fingers plunged into her flesh and brought forth a spray of blood, as she fell upon him.

He screamed with all the breath in his body, but no sound escaped his lips. His hand had merged into her skin as if they were one body, and he could not pull himself free.

"Who is like God?" Alma clawed at his shirt while she cried out, spitting blood in his eyes.

"What! I don't know! I don't know! Nobody!" Michael sputtered, sounding as if he was underwater. He gasped, but he felt he could not get any air.

He tried to desperately shake himself awake as the walls crumbled, and Alma's face shrivelled and warped into a featureless facet of stone. She was removed from him, now. Though he knew he was dreaming, terror made him feel faint and feeble. Everything melted around him, and he was plunged into the darkness. The ceiling split and came crashing down.

And then he opened his eyes.

His face was buried deep in the pillows. He shot upright, drew in a relieving breath, and grasped at the linens, his legs, his arms. All was intact.

He lit a candle. The clock read half past two o'clock. It was dark outside. He had slept for over twelve hours. Deathly shrieks echoed in his ears as he pieced reality back together.

He felt dreadfully ill and disturbed, both by his dream and by all that had transpired yesterday. If only all of that had been a dream as well…

Nobody else was likely to be awake, so he rose up, washed his face in yesterday's cold water, and wandered around the house. Normally, he found the wee hours to be tranquil, and the darkness a soothing cover, but the air was eerie and desolate this morning. After that awful dream, he sought any signs of life.

Sophie was curled up around her kittens. Michael patted her head as he passed.

Alma was asleep on the couch in the parlour, with her face hidden in her sleeves and hair. He was not sure what he would say to her when she woke up. Nothing seemed good enough. Maybe he could write it down first, but where to begin?

There was a chill, so he started a low fire. All he could think to do now was sit and wait.

He'd never gotten to watch her sleep before. He always imagined he would get to see her drift off to sleep peacefully, feeling her breath on his neck and her head on his breast. Were her dreams more pleasant than his? Yet again, he wished the circumstances were different, and he could only blame himself.

How long did she weep? He would have wanted her to seek him for solace, but why should she have done so when he drove her away? His last words to her wouldn't leave his head. He let them stay, figuring that it was his punishment to be tortured by them.

A slash of blue cleaving the room into two halves let him know that dawn was upon him. Michael extinguished his candle and decided to make himself useful by putting on water to boil. He'd done it over an open fire before, but this was his first time making the attempt with a real stove. He spilled some of the water and was initially unsure of how to light the stove, but it was not disastrous. Perhaps it would please her to have a little less work to do when she woke.

The first to arrive was not Alma, but Dr. Webb. Michael heard him descending from the second storey, and he was overtaken by a sense of dread and foreboding. He almost felt an urge to hide himself. Maybe go for a walk.

He'd already been spotted.

"Michael!" the doctor called as he took out his pipe. "Just who I wanted to see!"

"Good morning, Dr. Webb," he answered feebly. "There is water on the stove."

"Ah, very good, very good," he sat down, leisurely stuffing his pipe as though he had all the time in the world. "Well, don't go anywhere right this minute, I'd like to have a word with you."

He could not have gone anywhere even if he wanted to. Apprehension riveted him to his chair.

"You have had a little tiff with Alma, then," he observed as he struck a match, painting his already stern features in harsh, flickering shadows.

288

"That is a word you could use, sir, yes."

"Hmm, I see. James found her quite beside herself yesterday, and she would not tell me what had pricked her for quite some time. It was only his recounting of you storming into your chamber that gave me any clue. Normally, I would not consider it to be any of my business, but when my children suffer, I think I should intervene no matter the circumstances. Especially Alma, as for all her grace and composure, she has always been so tender."

He had a draught of his pipe, undoubtedly delighting in the dramatic pauses that accompanied the action.

"Such is rarely found unbroken in this merciless world. There is even some of it in you… even if your current conduct does not align. She went to great lengths to absolve you of blame. What about you? What would you say for yourself?"

Michael's tongue had hardened like clay, and he could not seem to easily open his lips.

"You have grown into quite a bold and proud young man, don't you think, Michael?"

At that moment, he did not feel he was either one of those. It was beyond him to even speak.

"So, answer me."

"Sir, I am in error," Michael choked out with much effort. "And I have no excuse."

"Then I will not tell you what you should or should not do," Dr. Webb replied. "But I would advise you to make amends in due time. What will you say to her when she wakes up?"

"I... I don't know."

"Hmph. She said the same thing."

The kettle began to steam in that interval. The doctor rose from his chair and went to the stove.

"Would you have some coffee, Michael?"

"No thank you, sir."

Dr. Webb's calm and cool disposition scalded him worse than if he had been viciously reprimanded.

"Frankly, I feel shouting is rarely necessary, if at all," he continued, as if he had heard Michael's thoughts. "It does not make your point any clearer, and may only make people feel more inclined to tune you out. But when you speak softly, they must pay attention in order to understand you. It is better to be asked to speak up than be told to pipe down."

"That is sound advice, I'd say."

"Excellent. Make use of it."

"I will, sir. Sorry."

"Save your sorries for those you have wronged."

"S— yes."

Dr. Webb sat down with his cup. Alma entered behind him.

"Alma! There you are," he turned around in his chair and offered a bigger and brighter smile than had ever before graced his countenance. "I was worried you would catch a cold, sleeping out in the parlour! And how did you sleep?"

"Well," was all that she said as she helped herself to the coffee. "I will start preparing breakfast once I have awoken a bit more."

Michael stood and pulled out a seat for her. She did not take it, electing to sit beside her father instead. Not once did she lift her gaze off of the floor.

"Are you still rattled from yesterday?" he asked, immediately warned to change his tune by a frigid stare from Dr. Webb. "Mmm, that is, do you feel better?"

"I feel alright."

Nobody who said "I feel alright" had ever been alright.

Now what? Did he speak up now, or give her space for the time being?

His own nerves had turned on him, and chose the latter. Nothing he strung together sounded good enough in his head to be said aloud.

James came in as Alma began to cook.

"Good morning, James," Michael offered.

He flashed an obscene gesture behind his coffee cup. Understood.

She was the last to leave the table, because she pitifully pecked at her plate. Michael sat back down across from her, thinking that he now knew what to say.

"Alma," he tried, and she lifted her head but only barely held eye contact.

So she was at least responsive.

"You know," he reached a hand towards her but did not touch her. "I have been quite troubled… and stressed as of late."

"We've all been stressed," she leaned away from him.

"Yes, I—" he froze, because when he ventured to explain his thoughts and feelings at the time of his outburst, it all seemed so silly now… absurd, even.

"You what?"

"Ah… it's nothing, I suppose."

Again, he was tongue-tied. Why? All he had to do was say he was sorry, and the rest should have come naturally. And he was sorry.

This time it was Alma who departed, and he was the one who was speechless, and still, she was not the one at fault.

She retreated into work and studying once again. He shared the same habit. Still, it was bothersome when he wanted just a moment alone with her.

Perhaps he really just needed to relax a touch. After he did some work in the study and around the yard, he decided to take Alma's advice and read. He pored over the shelves in the parlour, looking for something that might have interested him.

A work of fiction would have been a pleasant change of pace from reading informational texts until his eyes crusted over. Maybe it was finally time to finish *Candide, ou l'Optimisme*.

He took it to the seat closest to the window.

Any practice or skill was like a muscle: that is, it tends to weaken when it is not exercised regularly. Michael had not read for pleasure in quite some time, so he did not imagine himself ploughing through half of the volume in one sitting as he might have done as a young boy, before his brain had turned to mush.

He found the narrative a bit dull at first, but he appreciated the almost amusing barrage of one misfortune after another. It was familiar to him…

Michael heard a metallic crash and the slosh of spilling liquid, followed by Alma's distressed chatter. He left the book on the side table and threw open the parlour door.

Apparently, she was scrubbing out the oven, and collided with James on her way to pour out the resulting bucket of black muck. His coat was soiled all down the front. Though he handled it well, Alma apologised continuously, which was what Michael should have done hours ago, and for something much more blunderous.

"I'll wash it soon, I promise!" she gathered it up and carried it to the sewing room. "I just have to deliver some letters before the post office closes!"

"It's dark already," Dr. Webb called to her from the stairs, having been drawn out by the noise. "I'd rather you not go out alone."

Michael was ready to volunteer, but Dr. Webb elected James to accompany her.

"No, Papa, it's quite cold, and his coat is all wet and dirty!"

"Take my coat, James," Michael offered by gesturing to it hanging on the stand. "I know it isn't ideal, but you're a mite taller than Dr. Webb, and it's better for it to be too big than too small."

He reluctantly took it and slipped it on, nearly swallowed by it, for he was a lanky fellow. Immediately, he wrinkled his nose and "discreetly" gave it a sniff.

"Alma just washed it, and I'm not filthy!"

James uttered what was likely a contrary statement under his breath as he walked out the door behind his sister.

"I suppose you could have gone with her, or for her," Dr. Webb noted. "But I think she still needs time to herself."

"How much time?" he sank into the seat he'd left behind.

"Just wait until she gets back. She will feel much more at ease and more patient once she has gotten all of her work finished," the doctor passed into the kitchen as he spoke. "On that note, I think I'll prepare dinner myself, since she's had much on her plate today."

Michael knew the wait was going to be agonising, but he consented. He ventured to read a little more, but he could not focus, and the lines merged together. Now he was restless and unable to sit in one place, especially while she was out in the cold, and the sun had set. He didn't even build up a fire where he sat, because he didn't feel entitled to one.

At around six o'clock, he heard a faint gunshot. This startled him, though it was not an uncommon occurrence out in the country. It just wasn't so typical to hear them in the direction of town…

The doctor was making a savoury suet pudding with dried herbs and mushrooms in a bourbon sauce. It smelled divine, and he was famished, but even that could not take his mind off of things.

It was completely dark before long. He wished he had gone with her anyway! Maybe he would go out and get them himself. She may have been displeased, but it would give him peace of mind knowing exactly where they were.

He searched in vain for his good coat, remembering *after* he tore apart his room that James had borrowed it. Well, that was fine. He threw on his grandfather's old coat, though it was a bit more cumbersome, and he was on his way.

He'd just crossed the porch steps when he spotted a handful of silhouettes slowly scaling the stile in the starlight. His heart leapt, for he knew it must have been them.

Michael gleefully bounded down the hill to meet them, and as he approached, he noted that it was not two, but three people, stumbling and struggling as though they were painstakingly hauling something among them.

"Hillo! Do you need help?" he asked.

The voice that answered him belonged to neither James nor Alma, but Mr. Briggs.

"Get the doctor! Be quick!"

Michael did not know what this was about, and though every cell in his body urged him to rush forward and see what was wrong, he forced himself to turn around and run right back across the lawn with all the speed that he might.

He tore through the hall and pulled Dr. Webb away from his pudding without taking no for an answer. He himself extinguished the stove and dreaded what would be brought into the light.

His heart just about stopped when James and Alma were dragged inside, covered in blood and barely conscious.

XIX

"*ALMA*!" Michael howled and lunged for her, but he was elbowed away by Dr. Webb.

"Away! Don't shake her, she has hit her head."

"What do I do? What do I do?" he shook the doctor instead.

"Nothing. Stand to one side, but stay close. You may be needed later."

Michael stood and helplessly watched the two men take Alma and her brother into the sewing room. He fetched anything that they asked for and brought it with trembling hands. Now, he had a good look at them. They were covered in bruises and scrapes.

James had a broken nose and right hand, and his left shoe was missing, along with Michael's coat.

Alma's nose was also broken, and she had a nauseating gash on her lovely forehead that bled profusely. Her bodice was ripped down the front, and her eyeglasses were gone.

This wasn't a slip on the ice. They'd been attacked.

Dr. Webb first sponged away the blood, and spoke to them continuously to keep them awake and alert. How could he be so calm?

Mr. Briggs was the one who brought them there, so Michael latched onto him and began to interrogate him at once.

"Briggs, what happened to them?" he demanded. "Who did this? Where are they? What happened, what did you see—"

"Now, Mr. Bennett!" he brushed Michael off and took him quite firmly by the arms. "I did not see a lot, but I definitely 'eard plenty."

"Tell me, then! Tell me, please!"

"Well, what I remember," he began in a strain that was articulate, but intolerably slow. "I was wiping down the counters in me establishment, as I do, and I heard so much shouting, and many shuffling feet. So I grab me gun, and I run out to see what the fuss is at this hour. And I see two large men 'ad drug the Webbs into the alleyway. My, the little one shouted and shouted!" pointing a thumb at Alma. "And it's a good thing, too, hor I might not've come out. Fought like a wet cat, too. But I fired a warning shot, and the rats scattered to the wind. I reckon they aren't in mortal peril, but they were beat badly enough that I didn't fancy they could get hon 'ome without 'elp. I say, it's fortunate that they 'ave a doctor living close by!" he gave a hearty chuckle at the end of his speech.

For a single second, Michael was incredulous that the man could joke at a time like this, but everybody had their own manner of handling a difficult situation.

The more he heard, the more he was grateful for an honest fellow like Mr. Briggs, but his heart sank more and more with every detail.

"Why would anyone attack them?" he asked, scared to death that he already knew the answer. "What did they have on them?"

"I certainly couldn't say. Didn't find anything valuable on them, but that don't mean much, I suppose."

"Mr. Briggs, thank you," Michael took his hands and led him out of the sewing room. "Is there anything I can do for you while you're here? Would you like anything?"

"No, no thank you," he declined, but held onto Michael's hands all the way to the front door. "Nobody's tending to me tavern right this minute, I must be going. But do stop by and tell me how the young Webbs are gettin' hon. Tell me all about it."

"Yes sir, I will. Over a glass of whiskey, perhaps. Thank you so very much. Thank you, Briggs," Michael clung to him until he was visibly annoyed, then shut and latched the door behind him on his way out.

Dread weighed heavily upon him once more.

He went straight back to the Webbs and found James upright and talking with his father just fine, though with a bit of difficulty moving his mouth. It seemed he'd broken a tooth as well. Alma was absently running a finger over the stitches in her head. They both had fresh scarlet and purple bruises all over their faces.

"What happened, James? Are you alright?" Michael knelt down beside Alma and tried to take her hands, finding her nails completely destroyed.

"Do I look alright to you, genius?" he spoke from one corner of his mouth. "These two damn lunatics snatched us up, and ol' Briggs drove 'em off. Didn't see their faces, but Alma scratched one of 'em up nicely and got some of his hair. We'll probably send it off to see what can be done with it."

If Michael's worst suspicions were confirmed, probably very little.

"Oh… and your coat's gone. Couldn't be helped, really."

His coat… *his coat*…

"You two had better eat something," Dr. Webb rubbed his eyes and began tidying up his equipment. "And most definitely get some sleep."

He left the room and made his way upstairs. Michael did not want to leave Alma for even one second, but he followed the doctor to his study to see what he could coax out of him.

"Dr. Webb!" he called as he seized his coat. "Will they be alright? Do you have any idea why this happened?"

He lowered his head and kneaded his weary brow.

"I'd say, because you wear such a fine coat, some criminals saw them as a target for theft, but James says they didn't try to take anything from them. Best I can figure," he curled his lip as if the very idea sickened him. "They wanted Alma."

"Do you think we should go to the authorities?"

"I will. Tomorrow."

After a moment of silence, Dr. Webb added:

"If I had gone instead—"

"If you had gone instead, it might have been you who'd been thrashed! And I dare say, you can't easily tend to yourself! And if Alma or James had been hurt alongside you, you'd scarcely be able to help!" Michael interrupted, though even he was thinking that maybe the outcome would have been more favourable if he, himself, was present.

"Hmph. Well, I suppose you have a point."

"Now… are they going to be alright?"

"Most likely. They will just need rest. But I am a bit concerned about Alma's head, and I think she should be monitored throughout the night."

"I will do so, sir, gladly," Michael released the doctor's coat. "You must get some rest yourself, and be alert in case you are needed."

"Well, I really don't know if I could sleep," he admitted. "But I can certainly try. You must stimulate Alma every hour or so while she is sleeping and see if she stirs. Do look after James a bit as well."

"Yes of course!" he was already halfway down the stairs, not waiting to be dismissed.

He crossed paths with James, who was strangely eating pickled vegetables straight out of the jar, when there was a perfectly good pudding on the stove.

"James, I'm sorry about what happened—" he began.

"Don't apologise to me, fool, apologise to Alma! You still haven't yet; I don't know what she sees in you."

"I often wonder the same thing," he went to look for her. "Well, get better soon, ol' boy."

"Climb into a liquor bottle and pickle yourself, you soggy pencil outline of a man."

Under normal conditions, a young man would have been looking for a fight with that attitude, but this was neither the time nor the place, and Michael felt that the remarks were warranted, anyway.

Alma's bedroom door was ajar. He probably risked life and limb going inside, but he let himself in anyway. The room was simple but charmingly furnished, with lace curtains and polished woodwork, and a desk piled with haphazard heaps of books, pencils, and papers. None of that concerned him at the moment, as he was not looking to examine the room itself, but its infirmed inmate.

She was lying still and serene as a timeless marble statue. Even seeing her in that way wrung bitter tears of remorse out of him, and he threw himself at the side of her bed.

Now that the imminent danger had passed, Michael could not keep himself all together, and he choked and huffed, wracked by convulsions from the effort of restraint so that he did not wail.

"Alma… " he called in a hoarse whisper, with his lips against her cheek. "You're alright, Alma, you're alright. It's alright," he spoke just as much to himself as he did to her, but whether she would fully recover or not did not signify, because it absolutely was not alright. He caused this to happen, he was sure.

The eyelids fluttered. That was good, right?

She very slowly turned her face towards him in a succession of stiff, cog-like movements, and her eyes half opened.

"Alma!" he wanted to gather her to him and cradle her in his arms, but he had to settle for holding onto her hands. "Alma, I'm sorry about this. I'm sorry about everything! Everything, Alma! Oh, I'm sorry!"

Her eyes closed again. Was she asleep this whole time? Could she hear him?

"My nose," she murmured at last.

"What? Yes, your nose. What about it?" Michael's first instinct was to give the nose an affectionate nudge, but he refrained, as it looked sore and tender.

"It's broken… maybe it will match yours."

He couldn't stop himself from chuckling at that in spite of himself.

"I don't think it would ever resemble mine, Alma."

"I think… they wanted to rob us. I was not wearing your ring. They didn't take your ring."

Oh, the ring! He'd still kept it in its compartment ever since it'd been fixed, because she'd asked him to "hold onto it" and never came to him to retrieve it.

"*Your* ring," he corrected her. "On that note, I'll be right back."

He leapt up and made a wild dash to his room. He knew exactly where it was and tore it out of its parcel.

"Your ring! Here it is," he presented it to her and placed it on her little hand, where it was supposed to be.

"Hmm… " she lifted her hand up to have a look. "Opals and pearls… they're bad luck. Even when I wasn't wearing it, this happened to me."

"Do you not want it anymore?"

"Of course I do," she hid her hand in the folds of the sheets, as if afraid he might try to take it. "I'm tired… I'm very tired…"

"Sleep. I'll watch you."

"Ah… I might not wake up."

Those words made him feel weak, and he felt as though his heart might crack apart, knowing she thought such ghastly things.

"You will wake up, Alma! You will be well
soon, and much faster if you get plenty of rest.
Nothing will happen to you. Go to sleep."

Michael lightly traced his fingers over her face.
She seized his hand and dug her ragged nails
into it.

She shuddered exactly once, and squeezed her
eyes shut. Tears seeped from her lashes.

"I'm afraid. Don't let go of me, Michael."

It stung him horribly, but he steeled his breath
and kept himself composed.

"I won't, Alma. Go to sleep. Everything is
alright."

It's not alright. Stop lying to her, and to yourself.

Her grip slackened, and he brought her hand
down to rest at her bosom.

Michael was determined, this time, not to fall
asleep, and he would not fail. He watched her
tirelessly, and in two hour intervals, he would
gently coax her awake and chirp out jovial
remarks about how she had awoken after all,
then he would offer her a sip of water and allow
her to drop off again. Sometimes she was irate

about being woken up, but other times she was appreciative.

Even when morning came, he was in no danger of passing out, though his bones ached and creaked. It was surely nothing compared to her injuries. Dr. Webb came in at around five o'clock to carefully stroke her head and check her stitches, then he went to examine James.

"Michael," he turned around on his way out, and Michael saw that his eyes were so very red and drooping. "I don't think you've eaten at all since yesterday morning. If you would like to have breakfast, I'll take watch over her."

He really did not feel that he could eat anything, but it would not do to make himself ill from self-neglect, so he decided to force himself to have an appetite.

There was no chance of him properly reheating a steamed pudding, so he ate last night's dinner cold. It did not appeal to him, either because mushrooms are no good at room temperature, or because he was simply too anxious to savour it. Either way, he choked it down, and at once felt significantly less feeble, but still just as miserable.

As for Alma and James, they needed a hot breakfast. He found the resolve to use the stove when he considered that just some simple toast couldn't be that difficult. Surely even he couldn't ruin it beyond repair. He'd cooked game over a fire before. This couldn't have been that different.

Michael laid out unevenly sliced brown bread to toast when the oven heated up, and put water on the stove to boil for tea or coffee.

Some of the bread came out burnt on one side and undercooked on the other. He'd made the oven too hot and did not distribute the heat properly. He took a knife that was probably meant for cutting meat and generously slathered the toast in butter and blackberry jam. Not terrible for a first attempt.

He took a plate to James, who probably didn't touch it, and offered one to Dr. Webb as well. Now he had to wake Alma.

"Alma, here, I've made breakfast for you!" Michael pulled her into a semi sitting position and presented her with a tray of toast and tea. "I know you'd prefer coffee, but tea would perhaps be a bit milder."

She furrowed her brow, apparently sceptical of his attempt before she'd even fully opened her eyes.

"You made this?" she asked weakly, but a smile spread over her lips.

"Yes! It's nice and hot," he brought a piece up to her mouth. "Give it a try."

She took a pitiful bite and chewed so slowly, it was almost concerning. He'd hoped the jam would hide how burned it was.

"It's fine," she decided, taking it from him and having another bite. "Maybe I need to teach you how to properly use the stove."

"You need only to eat and not trouble yourself," he insisted.

But just as he said that, a deafening screech pierced through the tranquillity of the morning.

"ALMAAAA—" Ida wailed and tore her way down the hall, towards Alma's room.

Michael lunged from the threshold and seized her by the arm, ready to scold her and drag her away, but he curtailed his chastising when he saw genuine tears and distress shone in her features.

"Ida, settle down," he contained her by gently folding her up into his arms and pressing her face to his breast to mute her bawling. "I guess you know Alma is badly hurt, but calm down and don't strain her, or she won't get better."

"Let me see Alma! I want to see Alma!" she whined still and fought him, and he relented.

"Be quiet, child!" he warned as she ran into the bedroom.

Michael stepped aside and surveyed from a distance. Ida climbed into Alma's bed and threw her arms around her neck, but remained at a moderate volume and did not squirm about or disturb her injuries. Alma offered her a taste of her toast. Of course, she spat it out.

She probably would not hinder Alma's recovery, so Michael decided to leave them unattended and busy himself elsewhere.

The cats had not come out of their hiding place all this time. Last night's commotion must have startled them.

"Sophie," he whistled and rapped his knuckles on the floor by the stairs. "Come out, Sophie-Mama."

Michael must have looked like a maniac, perched on his hands and knees calling to a cat behind the staircase.

She poked her patchy head out, chirped at him, and then ducked back into her little corner. When she emerged again, she produced one of her kittens: a black and white male.

"Ho, what a big man you're getting to be!" he cupped the kitten in his hands and let him gnaw on his fingertips. The teeth were like dull needles. "I reckon you'll be a ferocious hunter before long!"

The remaining kittens came out to join the attack, and Sophie quietly trotted off while they were occupied. Cunning creature, making him a nursemaid while she slipped away undetected.

He laid himself out right there on the floor and allowed them to tramp all over him and chew up his clothes. At this age, cats were little different from dogs.

"My, you've lost your damn mind," James rebuked Michael and stepped over his legs on his way to the kitchen for more coffee. "Hopefully they devour you."

"James, I've made things right with Alma," Michael replied without lifting his head; there was a cat in his hair, so he could only strain his eyes. "And I will continue to do so. You needn't chide me. Let us be friends again."

"We were never friends. I've merely held my tongue for Alma's sake. She's always been soft and easily manipulated."

How could he speak of her in that way when she was in poor health? Was he really going to insult her just to make his point against him? Michael would have broken some of his teeth if somebody hadn't already done it for him.

Regardless, he stretched out his hand in a diplomatic gesture.

"Well, then let us be civil again. For Alma's sake."

James came out of the kitchen with his cup in his left hand, and glowered down at him as if he might trample him. Michael quickly remembered his bandaged right hand.

"Ah, right, yes. My mistake. But the sentiment remains."

He huffed and stepped back over him.

"Right," he muttered.

That was the most favourable response he could have hoped for, anyway.

Sophie went into Alma's room, and the kittens followed. Ida produced some squeals of delight at their arrival, but quickly silenced them, and was quiet from then on.

"Michael!" Dr. Webb called as he descended the stairs, looking around and finding the subject of his enquiries, then sporting a dumbfounded expression, probably not expecting him to be on the floor.

"Dr. Webb," he answered, now able to sit up with no trouble. "Did you need something?"

"As a matter of fact, I did," he continued his descent and held out a bundle of sealed documents. "I'd like you to deliver these to post. And then, when you come back… have you your rifle and pistol, still?"

"Ah, yes, sir, I have both," Michael answered coolly, though the question thrilled his nerves.

"Good. Make sure they are in serviceable condition."

It was plenty cold outside when he set out, but the wind blew from behind him, and he could ignore the chill as long as he kept walking. He found himself continuously thinking about Dr. Webb's request, and he was quite ahead of him. Ever since the incident with Albert Gillman,

Michael had kept his pistol close at hand, and his rifle always by his chamber door.

After posting Dr. Webb's letters, he decided to stop by Mr. Briggs's inn, but he was not prepared for what he saw.

Michael ran towards the inn when he spied shards of glass littered around its facade, and when he came closer, he found the windows smashed, bottles broken open, a free flow of ruined liquor, and the furniture destroyed.

"Briggs!" he shouted into the mess. The innkeeper emerged from a door behind the tavern's counter.

"Bennett! You're ha sight for sore eyes, yes indeed," his manner was jovial, but his countenance was woeful and frantic.

"What happened here, Mr. Briggs?" Michael let himself in through the door, though the large windows were, of course, wide open. He was not completely uncivilised, unlike whomever had passed through recently.

"It's hawful!" said Briggs, which was apparent to Michael already. "Last night, some 'eathens vandalised the tavern! They ruined most o' me stock, as you can see, they just about razed the place! I imagine those criminals were furious with me for thwarting them."

I imagine they were furious with me, not necessarily with you.

He continued.

"Some men be comin' by today to assess the damage, but least I 'ad some good stock stored up in the cellar. Can I get you something to drink?" he asked with a genuine earnestness, as if carrying on with his job was his only comfort.

"Sure, since I'm here. Let me have some of that whiskey we discussed, if you've got it."

Mr. Briggs served him gladly, and he sipped his drink standing at the counter while they fretted over the damages, and all that had taken place the night before. Briggs had a drink himself as he recounted the details. And another. And another. Briggs was usually such a phlegmatic fellow, that it was truly distressing to witness his sorrowful state.

After finishing his whiskey, Michael ran back to the house and returned out of breath, with a cheque for two hundred pounds (originally three, but quite shamefully, he scrapped that note), and Briggs was even more difficult about it than Dr. Webb. He was in tears when he finally accepted.

Even then, since he was staunchly opposed to taking handouts, Michael had to take his best bottle of liquor and call it a very elaborate purchase.

"But you didn't get it from me," Michael insisted in a hushed voice, trying to shift himself to block the transaction from view. "You didn't get it at all, as far as anybody other than your banker is concerned. Don't let anybody know that you have it."

"Oh, Michael Bennett!" he wept, and quickly lowered his voice at Michael's behest, opting instead to come close and tearfully whisper in his ear. "I say, I won't forget this for as long as I live! There hisn't a more tender and generous man on this earth!"

"I wouldn't be so sure of that. Anybody with the means to do so would surely be glad to repay you for your service to this town."

Michael left in high spirits that were dragged back down almost as soon as he stepped out into the streets.

He expected Gillman's associates to retaliate, but he apparently overestimated their stoutheartedness. Of course they were cowards, and would not engage him directly.

*Well, I'm out here in the open, and unarmed.
Come and get me if you will. Skin me alive.
Shoot me dead. Drag my body through the mud.
Hang me from a tree.*

Naturally, nobody accosted him right then and there, but he caught whispers through the heavy air, commenting on the random series of crimes that had recently plagued the streets, and their wandering eyes fixed on him, the eccentric newcomer. They talked about how they were afraid to send their children to school, and some even shrank away when he passed.

They would be correct to cast their blame in his direction. All of this was his doing.

He never fancied himself a righteous man. He was just a man that tried to do what he thought was right at that moment, and was often so very wrong…

As for his reputation, he was never revered or adored in this town, but he was respected and recognised. The trust he'd worked hard to build up over many months was crumbling away.

At the house, he put the bottle in the kitchen, then readied his weapons and went to Dr. Webb to see what his plans for them were.

"Well, I tried to contact the authorities already," he explained, with his back turned, and his gaze fixed on some point out the window. "But they told me they would not hear the case unless I sent the hair sample to an unbiased laboratory and could confirm it even belonged to a person."

"That isn't right!" Michael protested, but this corruption confirmed his fears even further.

"It is not, indeed. And I think that means they are knowingly protecting somebody within their own ranks, though I consented to reach out to a laboratory regardless. That said, I've considered the possibility that they will be back. Here soon, I will send James and Alma to their mother's house and request a member of the church accompany them safely. They will most likely be secure there, as very few people here know where Mrs. Webb lives."

"And what else, sir?"

"Well, I will be requesting an investigation from a much higher jurisdiction," he turned to face Michael, with his face shadowed over. "And if I see any living thing on my property that I don't recognise, I'm shooting it."

His expression and voice were both hard and cold as stone. Michael had almost forgotten that the doctor was a military man.

"So, you want me to keep a watch with you?"

"I would not ask you to stay here if you feel
unsafe doing so," said he. "But if you will, you
ought to be armed and possibly ready for a
fight."

Michael seriously considered this offer, and
pondered it all throughout the day, but he felt he
had caused enough trouble already, and
wondered if all of his friends would no longer be
targeted if he was not there.

Immediately, he cast aside that thought, because
it was agony. In the parlour, he sulked and
suffered over these ideas that intruded on his
illusion of peace, with a glass of fine brandy that
he sipped without tasting.

Ida came in, after an interval.

"What are you doing in here?" she climbed onto
his knee without his permission, and before he
could stop her.

"What are you doing *on me?* Off with you, I'm
not your father," Michael placed her on the floor,
no longer feeling the need to be patient now that
his personal space had been breached. "Has
Alma finally had enough of you?"

"She's sleeping, and she asked me to see where you went."

"Well, you've seen me. Now what?"

"You're going to take Alma away from me, aren't you?"

"What?" that, he did not expect to come out of her mouth, of all the nonsense she spewed. "What are you talking about? Alma is more devoted to you than just about anybody else in the world. How could I possibly?"

"She told me you were going to marry her, and that means she won't live here anymore. Why are you making her marry you?"

"Ida, Alma is her own person, with her own life. She agreed to marry me on her own accord. I cannot *make* her marry me. That is unlawful, and unnatural."

"Albert was going to marry me!"

Michael nearly choked to death on his last sip of brandy.

"He was not!" he sputtered and gagged. "You are far too young to marry, too young to even consider the idea."

"Julia was married at thirteen! I am almost twelve, a grown lady!"

"*Juliet,* I believe you mean to say. And look what that brought her!" he said this, but then immediately realised his error, as she probably had not read the source material and was only repeating the vile justifications that Gillman put into her head.

"It is legal, if my mother consents."

"It's also legal in China to mutilate young girls' feet, but it is undoubtedly barbaric. And suppose you were to have children," he winced at the bitter taste of those words. "At your age, you could be maimed, or worse. Do you even know what marriage entails?"

"You have a wedding in a church, and then go someplace far away, and you can kiss and drink ale."

Lord… Michael did not bother trying to correct her, as it was beyond him to do so, and she likely would not have listened to him.

"Alma will explain that sort of thing to you if you ask her. Ask her or Aunt and Uncle Webb, and only them. Nobody else," he set his glass on the table and wiped his mouth. "Anyway… why would you be in such a hurry to be an adult, Ida?

You have many years ahead of you. There is no rush."

"If I'm an adult, I can do whatever I want."

"You cannot do any such thing. Nobody truly can. There will always be consequences for your actions, and you will have obligations all of your life. Maybe your parents have not done what they could to prepare you for it, and I am sorry, but you are not ready for womanhood. Alma has been an adult for you all of this time, and it is no easy feat on her part."

"She does most things here. Uncle Henry says the house comes apart without her."

"That, it probably does," Michael remembered her prolonged leave last year, when the men of the house struggled to cook a presentable repast or even iron their own clothes. He was still unable to do either one. Beside that, the energy and life she brought to the home was unmatched, and everyone felt its absence now, while she was confined to her room. "But I think right now, she needs only to look after herself. We all owe her that."

That meant doing most things around the house by themselves, and not letting Alma inevitably try to get out of bed and do it. Dr. Webb clearly retained some semblance of domestic independence from his days as a bachelor, and James was at least competent enough to wash his own coat. The same could not be said for Michael.

Ida adapted quickly, by asking everyone else to do most things for her. After much pestering, James prepared her two jam and butter sandwiches, and milk with honey. This seemed to be her way of satiating her cravings for sugar now that she had run out of money to buy sweets.

Additionally, it seemed she simply could not cope when somebody wasn't giving her their undivided attention, and she knew precisely how to get it. In about two hours, she stumbled into the parlour moaning like an old man in his death throes.

"You'd better be dying to be making noise like that!" Michael glared at her. "What's the matter?"

"I am dying! I'm sick! My insides feel like they're rotting, and I'm hot like I have a fever!"

"A fever? Well, come here and I'll see."

"Alma kisses my forehead to check my temperature."

"Not even if your life was at stake," he grumbled and bared his wrist to press against her face. "You are not even warm. You will likely live."

"But my stomach hurts so much!"

"No wonder! You ate nearly a whole jar of jam for dinner, and washed it down with more sugar! Go and have some water."

"I can't get it myself," she fell to her knees and threw herself on her face on the couch. "I feel so weak."

"Fine," he got up so he didn't have to fuss with her.

She spent the night in Mrs. Webb's room, surprisingly.

"Alma likes her bed to herself," she explained, displaying an astounding respect for somebody else's boundaries.

And how was Alma? She had scarcely left her room in nearly twenty-four hours. According to Dr. Webb, this was the threshold for which they would no longer need to constantly worry over her if she was still able to be easily awoken.

Her door was closed, so he tapped lightly on the frame.

"Come in. It's unlocked."

He found her sitting up in bed, with her hair in plaits, and kittens sleeping at her feet. The swelling of her nose had significantly diminished, but her face was still quite purple.

"There you are!" Michael took a seat at the foot of her bed. "How are you feeling? Has Ida run you absolutely ragged?"

"No, she has been quite solemn," Alma had to narrow her eyes nearly completely shut to focus on him without her glasses. He came closer. "She can be, when she wants."

"Which she seldom does."

A beaming smile graced her lips, and it drew him out of his gloom for a moment, but then he remembered all the more clearly that he would soon have to sever his heart strings, and likely damage hers in the process.

But for now, he had her near him, and could listen to her breath.

"I've not left my bed very often. How is everyone managing?"

"Well enough," he wanted to say that everyone suffered greatly without her bustling through the house, but she was supposed to be recovering and at ease.

She nodded.

"You know… I likely could have gotten up more. I've felt fit enough to do so… but this repose has been rather delightful."

"I'd say you've earned it. Take as much time as you need."

She held her arms out, and he gladly nestled against her. He kissed her as carefully as he could with her sore nose; he kissed her as fervently as he would if he knew he'd never see her again.

Because it was entirely possible that he wouldn't.

Without meaning to, he had fallen asleep at some point, and nobody came to wake him. He did not want to sleep. He wanted to be fully conscious to speak to her and look upon her as long as he could, but she was so warm, and his eyes betrayed him.

After a dreamless sleep, he awoke some time at night, with his head upon her bosom, and his feet on the floor. This was all that he'd ever wanted, but the euphoria was lost on him, as he knew he could not stay that way. She was asleep, so he tried to very gently extricate himself from her hands without waking her.

I am sorry, Alma. I may have no choice but to let go of you, for your own safety.

He looked around the house. All was still. If he hurried, he could surely leave undetected.

XX

Once again, he packed up all that he thought he could carry from his room, but this time his load needed to be lighter, so that he made as little noise as possible. He took his pistol and left his rifle; aside from his mother's locket, he left all of the jewellery.

He wanted to come back one day. He needed to, no matter what changed, but he also had to consider that anything could happen in that interval, however long it was.

It was now about four o'clock in the morning. He cautioned stroking Sophie's head as he passed, for he could not resist the urge.

"Goodbye, Sophie," he hissed. "Goodbye, wee Mama."

Michael crossed the kitchen with his shoes in his hands. Hopefully if there was a light creak, it would be attributed to the cats.

He'd just opened the side door when he was found.

"Michael? Where are you going?"

Alma was standing in the kitchen with a lit candle, wearing just her nightgown, looking ghostly and beautiful.

He could not bring himself to lie to her. How could he, carrying so much?

"I'm leaving this place, Alma."

She was about to lunge forward, but set the candle down first, and then came to him silently on her unshod little feet.

"Why? What's the matter? For how long? Has something happened?"

"Well, yes," it was hard to even look at her. "And I think it is best I leave."

"Take me with you, then!"

He set his belongings down so that he could hold her hands one more time, but stopped himself at the last second. It may have made things more difficult for them both.

"I can't do that. I don't even know where I'm going, and I will not uproot you. Ida needs you anyway."

She had come close and began unbuttoning her gown. Was she too hot? Did the collar chafe?

He realised what she was doing after the fourth button, and a burning, unbearable thrill throbbed at every nerve in his body. It seemed his entire life consisted of wishing the same things happened, but in a different situation.

"No, Alma," he lowered her hands to her sides and tore his eyes away from that trembling white flesh.

Her lips quivered. She was visibly injured by his rebuff, but what could he do?

"You don't want me?"

He wasn't sure what to say to her. He probably shouldn't have said anything.

He did anyway.

"I do," he admitted. "But you're not thinking clearly."

"I am."

"You know I need to leave."

"But for how long?"

"Until they stop pursuing me."

"Who *are they*, Michael?!"

"The magistrate's associates," he tried to explain as quickly as possible. "I'm sure they have been targeting everyone around me in retaliation, and if I'm gone, they will surely cease their attacks."

She opened and closed her mouth a few times, probably about to upbraid him, or tell him it was a terrible idea— if she even believed him— but it was the only idea he had.

"Will you write letters home when you are safe?" she asked desperately.

"I'll try," he answered, though at that moment, he was sure he would not live to see twenty.

"Well, if you really wish to leave, I cannot stop you," she relented, and stepped away. He could not see her well, but he could hear and sense her weeping, and he could not wipe her tears. "But… I will pray over your passage continuously."

"Don't pity me, and save your prayers for someone worthy of them," he ordered her, turning cold so that he could remain composed and steadfast. Well, it was better for her to have a bitter recollection of him than to pine for his tenderness all her life. "Scrub me from your memory and go to London, as you wanted. Goodbye, Alma. Get back in bed before you freeze."

Goodbye, James, Dr. Webb, and Mr. Briggs: Ida as well, he added silently, as he could not go to them himself.

He slipped out before Alma could say any more, and she did not follow.

Michael trudged through the soggy grass with his trunk, and just as he did last year, he stubbornly clattered through the fields, so that nobody would see him. All the while, he fought with himself, over whether or not it was too late to turn around, back into Alma's arms, or whether his plan was even viable. The cold helped numb his feelings so that he could press onward for a considerable stretch, until there was no turning back.

With nobody to see him, he wept and wailed so badly that he could hardly see ahead of him, and his knees threatened to give out. Before long, he couldn't feel his face, and his tears froze to his chin. It was not his muscles that failed him, but his waning resolve that sapped the strength from his limbs. Many times, he stumbled and hit the ground hard, and then he had to crawl and slowly lift himself up again. As it was the middle of winter, few creatures stirred around him, if any. He really was entirely alone. Worst of all, he didn't know exactly where he was going, and barely knew why. He only knew that he needed to leave.

Now the sun was a sliver over the horizon. Michael ventured back into civilisation only to seek the train station. He skirted its vicinity, unsure of exactly how long he would have to wait, and wanting to speak to as few people as possible.

All he could think to do was board a train home: to his real home. Just a glimpse would comfort him. At that moment, it was all he had left. Abraham would have taken him in without a second thought, but he did not want to burden the old man, and he could not even face him in the state he was in.

He continued to weep into his handkerchief on the train, no longer caring who saw him do it. Nobody bothered him, but a tiny elderly woman told him "keep your chin up, sweet pea," not knowing his plight, or anything about him, and never seeing him again.

He departed from the train that same day. Now, it was certainly too late to go back. He would look like a fool, though a part of him was alright with that. He wanted to be Alma's fool.

That was behind him, now.

It was a beautiful, shining winter evening. The brilliant sunset painted the trees a myriad of soothing colours, and the hills were greyish purple.

If he caught a ride from town, he would need only to cross the thick, ornate treeline surrounding Ashwood, and then he could have just the one glance he needed. There would still be enough light for him to see it. The prospect raised his spirits the slightest bit.

He managed to find somebody who would take a strange, raggedy young man to Ashwood for a pretty penny. How eager he was! Finally, he had something to look forward to, no matter how small. Anticipation made him nimble, and he scaled the great hill with enthusiasm and vigour, as if ascending the stairway to heaven. Soon, only the treeline stood before him. The roof of the mansion shone in the last rays of the sun.

Michael fell to his knees.

The fine shrubbery and climbing vines were overgrown. The intricate mosaics on the walks had been lifted out of the ground, and even the fountain in the front garden was gone. The walls surrounding the perimeter were sinking and crumbling, after such a short time. Peering through the grand windows, he saw the curtains were stripped. It seemed everything that wasn't essential to its structural integrity was removed, and the rest left to rot.

Ashwood Hall was a disembowelled skeleton.

If this was how they treated the main house, he didn't want to imagine how the smaller properties had fared.

He was too beside himself to even cry out in despair. The soul had gone from the house, and he felt some of his had been taken with it. His sweetest memories of youth faded away. Everything he had pined for was gone.

He felt as though he had gone to war and left his lover at the mercy of the enemy. He had done this. Now, he looked upon a murder victim.

And would his gaze raise her from the dead and restore the light in her windows? Staying at the scene was only self-flagellation.

All there was for him to do now was walk. He carried on numbly, not yet ready to brave these sickening feelings.

Michael wandered through one of the family cemeteries. He passed between the graves of his parents, and he froze in terror when he stepped upon that round little stone. Now he knew exactly what it was.

He collapsed at the grave of his father and seethed with the anger and resentment he had repressed for many months.

"You told me to live with no regrets, just as you have!" he snarled at the lifeless slab of stone. "How could you place that burden on me, knowing all you had left me to handle alone? Did you really have no regrets? Are you watching me from heaven with none still? Can you really be that cruel? If you regret nothing, then you feel nothing! You flung me onto the world with no knowledge and no means! You failed me and my sister! You wouldn't even say her name! Henry Webb has been more of a father to me than you, my own blood! Now I am torn away from him, and have only *you!*"

Michael knew he was needlessly shouting into the darkness, as there was nobody there to listen or answer. He was not entirely sure there was a heaven at all.

He added, after a stretch of silence:

"And I am no better. I have failed, as well. That, I cannot blame you for."

He shouldered his belongings and kept walking, like an automaton, towards the nearest town.

He walked, and walked, and walked, as he couldn't feel his feet anymore— drawn, as a moth, to the distant lights. He no longer cared who perceived him.

There was a tavern at the far end of the first street, so he went inside. It was full of a few drunken old men, and many beautiful women baring their shoulders despite the cold, leaning over the tables so that the tops of their breasts showed.

While he drank as much as the money in his pocket would allow, he thought he might take any company he could get, but when he approached them, he could not even speak, and only stared at them until they grew tired of him and left. One of them even puffed a mouthful of damp smoke into his face in order for him to take a hint. If he was not seeking their *service*, he was a waste of their time. Waking up in a strange woman's bed did not appeal to him. At the time, very little did.

Just by approaching them, he felt he had done a terrible thing, and he could only think of Alma. He wondered what she was doing now. Had she already forgotten him? He half hoped that she did. As for him, she would not leave his head.

He sought her in every woman he looked at, and thought he could become intoxicated until he saw a glimmer of her likeness, but to no avail.

After a stretch, they refused to serve him any more, and he stumbled out, almost unable to hold himself upright, too dazed to even weep anymore. He bumped into just about every person on the pavement, bringing a tirade of threats and swearing upon him as he ambled by.

A few of the people he passed asked for money, but he had none left in his pocket. In a trance, he handed his watch to a raggedy little mother with a baby on her back, and shuffled onward without waiting for thanks or reproach. He couldn't speak. He could hardly even think. It grew colder by the minute, and he did not feel it, unaware of the passage of time, or where he was.

Michael dreamed even as he walked. He saw what he'd left behind, and every mistake that led him to where he was. As always, he didn't see the full extent of his missteps until it was far too late, and because of that, he saw no reason to contemplate it now.

Suddenly, he felt tremendously light— he'd dropped his belongings. As he very slowly turned around to go back for them, he lost his footing and fell hard, spilling onto the pavement and landing on his side with a sharp, stabbing pain in his chest. His arms had failed to catch him. It startled him, and for a fleeting moment, he writhed and fought fruitlessly to sit erect, but still, his limbs would not cooperate. Once the primal, animalistic fear passed through him, he felt content and comfortable, wrapped in warmth, unwilling to struggle, with alcohol coming back up to burn his throat.

This is where I die, he thought, as his eyelids turned to lead and his breath staggered. *I don't know where I will go next, but anywhere must be better than here. Nothing of value will be lost to the world. If nobody will weep for me, then I won't, either.*

The whistling wind and distant voices swirling around him were a blissful lullaby. The pain in his side softened into a dull throb that was almost pleasurable. He did not feel the cold, but it chilled his lungs and plagued him with violent coughing fits that made him feel sleepy. Is this how his father felt in his final moments? Would he meet him again after this came to pass? Should he embrace him or spit in his eye?

Footsteps came close and fast, but he was too far gone to care. They faded away as quickly as they approached. He was pretty sure somebody had stepped on him, too.

An endless expanse of black bloomed in his eyes like roses in springtime, and it soon gave way to a warm golden light; at its centre, Alma— or an angel of her likeness— stretched out her arms to receive him, with her hair and gown billowing. By some miracle, heaven was real, and this undeserving soul was welcomed in. He felt light as a morning breeze, bright and new as the sunrise.

He reached out to touch her, and waited to be lifted away, but she snatched him by his coat and shook him violently, and the warmth he delighted in swelled into hellfire devouring his body.

"Wake up! Wake up!" the apparition cried, and suddenly, his body had weight again. "Sir, please wake up!"